ALSO BY
LAUREN WOLK:

Wolf Hollow
Echo Mountain

BEYOND the Bright Sea

by LAUREN WOLK

PUFFIN BOOKS

PUFFIN BOOKS

An imprint of Penguin Random House LLC, New York

First published in the United States of America by Dutton Children's Books,
an imprint of Penguin Random House LLC, 2017
Published by Puffin Books, an imprint of Penguin Random House LLC, 2018

Puffin Books & colophon is a registered trademark of Penguin Books Limited.
Visit us online at penguinrandomhouse.com

LIBRARY OF CONGRESS CATALOGING-IN-PUBLICATION DATA IS AVAILABLE.

Puffin Books ISBN 9781101994870

Printed in the United States of America

Edited by Julie Strauss-Gabel
Design by Anna Booth
Text set in Adobe Garamond Pro

14 16 18 20 19 17 15 13

For my father, who first took me to sea

The Elizabeth Islands,
off the coast of Woods Hole, Massachusetts.
1925

PROLOGUE

*M*y name is Crow.

When I was a baby, someone tucked me into an old boat and pushed me out to sea.

I washed up on a tiny island, like a seed riding the tide.

It was Osh who found me and took me in. Who taught me how to put down roots, and thrive on both sun and rain, and understand what it is to bloom.

The island where we found each other was small but strong, anchored by a great pile of black rock that sheltered our cottage—a ramshackle place built from bits of lost ships—nestled on a bed of earth and sea muck, alongside a small garden and the skiff that took us wherever our feet could not.

We didn't need anything else. Not in the beginning.

At low tide, we could cross easily to the next island, Curry-hunk, through shallows strewn with bootlace weed and minnows.

At high tide, the cottage sat so close to the risen sea that it felt nearly like a boat itself.

For a long time, I was happiest when the water rose and set us apart, on our own, so just the two of us decided everything there was to decide.

And then, one night when I was twelve, I saw a fire burning on Penikese, the island where no one ever went, and I decided on my own that it was time to find out where I'd come from and why I'd been sent away.

But I didn't understand what I was risking until I nearly lost it.

Chapter 1

I'll never know for sure when I was born. Not exactly.

On the morning Osh found me, I was just hours old, but he had no calendar and didn't much care what day it was. So we always marked my birth on whatever midsummer day felt right.

The same was true of my other milestones: moments that had nothing to do with calendars.

Like the day Mouse showed up at our door, whisker thin, and decided the cottage was hers, too. Much as I had.

Or the first time Osh let me take the tiller of our skiff while he sat in the bow and let the sun coddle his face for a while, his back against the mast, the fine spray veiling him in rainbows. Or the ebb tide when a white-sided dolphin stranded on our shore, Osh gone somewhere, and I came back from Cuttyhunk to find her rocking and heaving, her cries babylike and afraid. I used my bare hands to scoop away the wet sand that stuck her fast. And

I grabbed her crescent flukes and tugged, inch by inch, until the water lifted her enough so we both slipped back suddenly into the sea.

She looked me in the eye as she passed, as if to memorize what I was at that moment. As if to say that I should remember this, too, no matter what happened later.

None of which had anything to do with calendars.

Still, I know I'd lived on that tiny island for eight years before I began to be more than just curious about my name. The dream that woke me, wondering anew about my name, was full of stars and whales blowing and the lyrics of the sea. When I opened my eyes, I lay for a minute, watching Osh as he stood at the stove, cooking porridge in a scabby pot.

I sat up and rubbed the sleep from my eyes. "Why is my name Crow?" I asked.

When Osh stirred the porridge, the spoon made a sound like a boat being dragged across the beach. "I've told you," he said. "You were hoarse with crying when you washed up here. You cawed over and over. So I called you Crow."

That answer had always been enough before. But it didn't explain everything. And everything was what I had begun to want.

"In English?" I asked.

Osh sometimes spoke in a language I didn't know, his voice like music, especially when he prayed, but also when he painted his pictures of the islands and the sea. When I first asked Osh about it, he said that it was one of the few things he'd kept from life before the island. Before me.

Even though he did not speak it often, that other tongue flavored his English so he sounded different from everyone else. Miss Maggie called it his accent. But I thought maybe it was everyone else who had an accent.

"No, not English at first," he said. "But people here speak English. So: Crow."

I stood and stretched the night out of my bones. My arms, in the thin morning light, looked almost nothing like wings.

But when I stepped onto a stool in front of our mirror—just big enough for a face—I could see the resemblance in the curve of my nose. The birthmark on my cheek that looked like a little feather. My hair, darker than anyone else's. My dark eyes. My skin, like Osh's after six months in the sun.

I looked down at my skinny legs, my bony feet.

Plenty of other reasons to be called Crow besides the way I had once cried.

Osh, himself, had three names. Daniel: what Miss Maggie called him. The Painter: what the summer people called him. Osh: what I had called him since the time I could make words out loud.

His real name was complicated. Difficult for a small child to say. "Osh" was all I'd been able to manage. And Osh was what I'd called him ever since.

"I wish I knew what my real name was," I said.

For a long moment, Osh was still. "What do you mean by *real*?" he said.

"My real name. The one my parents gave me."

Osh was again silent for a while. Then he said, "You were brand-new when you arrived here. I don't know that you ever had a different name." He scooped some porridge into a bowl. "And if you did, I don't know how we'll ever learn what it was."

I fetched two spoons. "What it *is*, you mean."

When Osh shrugged, the hair that lay on his shoulders rolled up like night waves. "Was. Is. Will be." He filled a second bowl. "It doesn't much matter, since you're here now. And you have a name."

The sound of the porridge *thwup*ping into the crockery, the *tock* of the wooden spoon against the edge of the bowl, made me wonder who had named those things. And everything else in the world. Including me.

I could feel my curiosity strengthening, as if it were part of my bones, keeping pace with them as I grew.

But more than that—more than simple curiosity—I had a nagging need to know what I didn't know.

I wanted to know why there were pearls tucked inside some of the Cuttyhunk oysters but not others. I wanted to know how the moon could drag the ocean in and out from such a distance, when it couldn't stir the milk in Miss Maggie's tea. But I *needed* to know, among other things, why so many of the Cuttyhunk

Islanders stayed away from me, as if they were afraid, when I was smaller than any of them.

I wondered whether it had anything to do with where I'd come from, but that didn't make any sense. What did *where* have to do with *what*? Or *who*?

Something, yes. But not everything.

And I needed to know all three.

Osh didn't. When I asked questions about pearls or tides, he did his best to answer them. But when I looked beyond our life on the islands, he became the moon itself, bent on tugging me back, as if I were made of sea instead of blood.

"I came a long, long way to be here," he once said when I asked him about his life before the one we shared. "As far as I could get from a place where people—where my own brothers— jumped headlong into such terrible fighting that no one could see a thing through that bedlam. And for what? Over what?" He shook his head. "Over nothing worth the fight. So I refused to be one of them. And here I am. And here I'll stay."

While I waited for Osh to bring our porridge to the table, I tried to think of another name that suited me well, but I came up with nothing better than Crow, which I already had.

And it pleased me that I was named for a bird that was smarter than most. Smarter, even, than some people. So different from the gulls and fish hawks that wheeled and dipped over the islands that I felt a certain kinship with the big, black birds that drifted over from the mainland like lost kites, tipping to and fro in the wind before settling noisily in Miss Maggie's hornbeam tree. They didn't seem to belong on the islands. And sometimes I felt like I didn't, either. But we were islanders, nonetheless, no matter what anyone else might think.

Osh called me other animal names from time to time. Cub. Kit. Mule when I was stubborn. Wren when I was good.

Now and then, he called me a mooncusser, too, because I liked to scour the shore at night for whatever the tide had brought in, but I did not lure the ships that wrecked off Cuttyhunk, and I was no thief afraid of being moonlit as I searched for lost treasure. I had never cussed the moon.

But for the most part, we didn't rely on names. If we were apart, we were far apart, beyond calling. If we were together, we talked the way people talk when there's no one else. Names didn't matter much.

Chapter 2

Osh had built our cottage from whatever he could wrestle off the nearest shipwrecks that were slowly settling into the seabed, breaking up in storms, and otherwise disappearing, bit by bit.

The rest of the house was flotsam that had come to him, floating in on the tide, as I had, sometimes into our own little cove, sometimes on Cuttyhunk, where no one else wanted it.

He'd built the frame from long beams, the roof and walls from decking, the chimney from a vent pipe off a lost steamer, one window from a porthole. Our door was a piece of keel. Our hearth, a hatch lid. Our table a crow's nest turned upside down.

Osh had salvaged, too, many things that had no purpose but to be dear to us. The finest of these, two figureheads—solemn women with long, flowing hair——stared at us from either side of our fireplace, never blinking. And a pair of sun-white whale ribs arched over our doorway, a tarnished ship's bell hanging from their pinnacle.

And I'd found my share of baubles while searching the wrack line. Bits of sea glass among the mermaids' purses and limpet shells. A brass money clip with an elephant pressed into its face, all of it a crusty green. A banjo clock that would never again keep time but had a tiny cupboard where I kept the other trinkets I'd found. Another thing I had in common with crows: our habit of prizing the poorest of riches.

When I asked him what he'd done with the skiff that had brought me ashore, Osh told me he'd busted it up for firewood and burned it to keep me warm that first winter. For a long time, before I knew better, I wondered why that—of all the wood he'd salvaged—had ended up in the fire rather than our home.

With the money he made from lobstering and cutting ice out of Wash Pond and selling his paintings to the summer people, Osh had bought nails, a hammer, and whatever else he lacked. He dug clay from the sound side of Cuttyhunk, sailed it around to our cove, and mixed it with wood ash and salt to make the chinking that sealed the cottage against draft and hard rain. And he did everything else he could to make it strong and snug.

When I was old enough, I helped him keep it that way.

But even as we worked together on this home we'd made, I could not stop thinking about who had made *me*. Who had looked at me, soft and fresh as a blossom, and decided to give me to the tide. And why.

I carried those questions around with me like a sack that

got heavier as the years went by, even though I had become accustomed to the idea of it. Even though I was not unhappy with the life I had.

I just wanted to know. To understand. To put that sack down.

Some things I knew through and through.

Osh had told me many times—so often that it had become like a bedtime story—how he'd found me in an old skiff that had beached itself on the wrack line overnight. Had he not found me when he had, the incoming tide would have taken me back out again, to somewhere else. But he had wanted fish for his breakfast and had gone out to cast for a striper or two.

The skiff was barely seaworthy, but it had survived the trip to the island, even through the wild currents that wrecked much bigger boats.

What Osh expected to see when he came up to the little skiff I don't know, but it could not have been a new baby, lashed to the bench with strips of dirty linen, inches above the water that had seeped into the hull.

Osh told me how I stopped cawing and lay silent as a mouse when a hawk-shadow comes—I blinking up at him and he down at me—that morning when we first met.

He lived alone in a place that was difficult even for a grown man, but he took me in first before deciding what else to do with me. And I stayed.

He often told me how hard it was in those first days after I arrived. How he had traded lobsters for milk at the Cuttyhunk grocery, poured it in a little flask, and fashioned a nipple from a clam neck made to squirt seawater. I sucked salty milk from it, as if from the sea itself. He swaddled me in wind-softened sailcloth, washed me in a smooth sink in the rocks where rainwater collected. Tucked me up alongside him at night so we slept as one.

By the time Miss Maggie and the others found out about me, Osh had decided that I was his until someone else could prove otherwise.

Miss Maggie had tried for a while. Not, she said, to take me away. Only, she said, to make sure no one was searching for me. Perhaps, she said, my mother hadn't been the one to send me to sea. Perhaps, she said, my mother was pacing the shores across Buzzards Bay, her breasts swollen with milk.

So Miss Maggie bullied the postmaster until he sent word on his telegraph machine to ports from Narragansett to Chilmark, asking if anyone was looking for a newborn like me.

And she wrote letters, too, and sent them to places too small for a telegraph machine.

From some, she got no answer: Onset; Mattapoisett; even Penikese, though it was the closest.

And none of those who did respond knew of a missing baby.

But it didn't really matter.

By the time the replies made their way into Miss Maggie's hands, I'd already become Osh's. And he had become mine.

It was a mystery why the skiff had washed up on our little island and not on Cuttyhunk where most treasure and flotsam came to rest. But I was glad that it had.

I couldn't imagine that any of the other islanders would have fostered me had I drifted up on their piece of land. I thought it far more likely that they would have sent me off to the mainland, to some place without so much sea and sky. And that would have been a shame. Osh and I were surrounded by a wild world. And I preferred it that way.

Still, there were a few people on Cuttyhunk I liked well enough. And they seemed to like me in their odd way. But they never touched me. Never came close. Seemed content to know me from a distance. Which had been true from the very start— all I'd ever known from them—so I didn't question it much until I was older and began to pull on the loose threads in my life.

When I did that and everything began to unravel, a seam opened up and let in some light, which helped me see my life more clearly, but it also made me want to close my eyes, some-times, instead.

Miss Maggie was the only one on Cuttyhunk who did not seem to be afraid of me.

I was often sick as a baby and still too often sick as a child, and Miss Maggie was the only one to cross to our island with bread and soup and one of the potions she brewed from rose hips and nettle leaf. Hers was the only hand that had ever touched me, if I didn't count Osh or those who came before him, though I always did.

Despite all her hard work, her hands were as smooth as the inside of an oyster shell. When I asked her why, she frowned and told me that they were soft from the lanolin in the sheep's wool she sheared from her flock—or picked from the sheep that died in the rough—and spun into yarn. "But that doesn't mean they aren't strong," she said, as if I had doubted it.

When she put those hands on my hot forehead, I thought of sea lavender and April. But she hardly ever smiled, and when she talked everything came out with a hint of thunder in it. A little scolding, no matter what I'd done or hadn't done.

"You'll eat this soup and every spoonful," she'd growl. "You hear me?"

And I did eat every spoonful: No one else on Cuttyhunk made better soup than Miss Maggie did, with vegetables that came from the finest garden on the islands. She started her seedlings in hotbeds as soon as the sun was stronger than the snow and planted them out after the last thaw in a vast garden, rich with manure and sea muck: potatoes, celery, beans, cabbage, horseradish, snap peas, barley, melons, onions, cucumbers, tomatoes, and turnips.

If she spoke rough to *me*, she said softer things to her cows. And although they ate the same oats as all the other Cuttyhunk cows, hers gave the best milk on the island, so her butter was the best, too. And she made her hens so happy with marigolds and barley that they laid like troupers and hatched out more chicks than any on the Elizabeth Islands. With the flour and oil she got from trading eggs, Miss Maggie baked bread that made me happier than if I'd had cake, which I tasted only once in a blue moon. I was almost glad to be sick if it meant her bread and soup.

"She does make good soup," Osh always said before she arrived and after she left. "But soup is just one thing."

Her bravery was another thing.

"Don't you worry that you'll get sick, too?" I'd ask her as I lay in bed, my head aching.

"I've been sick before," she'd say. "And I'll be sick again, with or without your help."

I liked that about Miss Maggie. How simple she made things seem.

Chapter 3

*M*iss Maggie lived in a smart little house apart from most of the other year-rounders, though with all her animals she was not completely alone. One bad winter (though I don't know that there was ever a good one), she brought the smallest pig into the house with her and, when spring came, had to drag him back to his pen. When a half dozen wild turkeys froze in the sassafras trees alongside her barn, she carried them inside, one by one, like big, ugly babies, wrapped them in flannel, stood them by the fire, and fed them hot whiskey and milk. Every last one survived, and they neither pecked nor harried her when the thaw was complete, but simply walked out her front door into the sunshine the next day.

Four of her rabbits did not fare so well. Though she rescued their frozen bodies from the hutch and fed them the same strong drink, they revived for just a while before dying once and for all, so she skinned them and made them into a mighty stew with carrots from her root cellar and bacon from her smokehouse.

"It was the best stew I ever made," she said, "and I ate up every bit of it, but I was sorry for the way those poor rabbits died."

Then she lined her coat with their pelts and was much the warmer for it.

Mouse had a fur coat, too, and I loved to bury my face in it. To listen to the rumble in her chest.

Like Osh and Miss Maggie, she was not afraid to let me touch her.

We called her Mouse because that's what she said over and over again when she was hungry.

She settled for scraps of fish and a little of the jerky that Osh made from beef and blueberries. Or the fish heads that the Cuttyhunk men tossed back into the sea after cleaning their catch.

Sometimes she brought us a gift—once it was an eel that wriggled and rolled when she dropped it at my feet and that we all three ate in a stew—but usually she was too hungry to be proud of herself. All three of us were skinny. All three of us ate what we had, and we didn't think about what we didn't have.

Mouse was an obliging cat most of the time, but when Osh pinned her between his knees and trimmed her longest fur for his paintbrushes, she squirmed and yowled so pathetically that I mashed my hands over my ears and looked away.

"I'm not hurting her," Osh said as he carefully cut what he needed. "It'll grow back."

"Why don't you use your own hair?" I asked.

"I do," he said. "But fur is better for some things."

After he had harvested the bits that were longest—and farthest away from her claws—Osh spent a moment plowing through her remaining fur, yanking ticks as he found them. Some were as big as peas.

He gave them to me to smash on the rocks.

The first time I ever did that, small starbursts of Mouse's blood remained, so from then on I set them adrift on the current instead.

When Osh released her, Mouse shot out of the house like her tail was on fire.

"Why don't you just *buy* some brushes?" I asked.

Miss Maggie could order almost anything from the mainland, and she sometimes sent for things Osh couldn't buy from the Cuttyhunk market.

"This is free," he said, binding the fur to the tip of a brush handle. When he sculpted it to a point, such a brush would let him paint the pinfeathers of a young meadowlark or the petals of a wood lily.

But he never took one tuft of fur from Mouse when winter came.

I confess that I myself was often cold during those long winters on the island with Osh. Of course I wished for fresh apples and strawberries when the entire world was white and gray and the ground was iron hard, but mostly I wished for shipwreck wood that would mean warm hands and feet in January.

I never asked for the wrecks that granted those wishes, though. And since there was nothing I had done to cause such things and nothing I could do to stop them, I didn't feel bad about salvaging what we could when ships came to grief in the waters off Cuttyhunk, so turbulent that they were known as the Graveyard.

You might think that we wished most fervently for gold or silver—and I have to admit that when I finally found some treasure of that sort I was glad, for many reasons—but we never found any cargo more precious than the blacksmith coal that we harvested from a ship after it foundered in an August storm. Every single one of the crew survived, which was cause enough for celebration, but we were happy, too, that the ship had wrecked in the shallows so that at low tide we islanders could walk out in our tall boots, pulling dinghies along behind, to load up as much coal as we could and ferry it back to shore. The tide brought more to us, littering the wrack line with chunks of it that we gathered like shell seekers who knew too much about frostbite.

We treasured that coal and used it sparingly so it would stretch into a second winter. Even in June, when the cold weather was a world away, I could sweeten any bad day by remembering that one amazing thing: Come winter, we would be warm.

No one who's ever been as cold as a New England islander in February would care more about gold than coal.

But when I learned from Miss Maggie that coal squeezed by the weight of the world turned to diamonds, I looked at it differently and wondered what other rough and simple stuff held the promise of something rare.

Coal wasn't the only treasure that turned up on the Elizabeths.

The ships that had wrecked in the Graveyard took plenty of cargo down with them, and not all of it was lumber or cotton or rum.

A few of the islanders had found real riches from time to time. A diamond necklace caught in a lobster trap. A gold ingot in the tines of a scallop rake. One man, pulling an anchor off Naushon, hooked an old crown that had been buried in the muck for a century. Another, clamming off Nashawena, found a huge silver belt buckle that he cleaned up and wore as proudly as the buccaneers who had once sailed these waters, some of them true pirates, though only one of them—Captain Kidd—had been known to hide loot or give it away instead of spending it.

He gifted a fortune to Mercy Raymond, on Block Island, just down the seaboard from us, filling her apron with gold and jewels simply because she'd been kind. And he buried more on Cherry Tree Field on Gardiners Island, not so far from Cuttyhunk, before Governor Bellomont sent it to England, proof that the captain was a thief, and not just of gold or silver.

Treasure comes in many forms, and Captain Kidd had prized them all.

Miss Maggie was happy with plain and simple, but she some-times spiced my geography lessons with talk of gemstones caught and kept—and sometimes buried—by pirates like the wily Wil-liam Kidd: African diamonds, Burmese rubies, Brazilian emer-alds, all of them forged by the alchemy of the earth's hot spots. So hard and resilient that they could last for centuries in the cold salt and sand of islands like ours.

Lots of people thought Captain Kidd might have buried loot on the Elizabeths, well within his stomping grounds, but no one who had gone digging for treasure out here had ever found any.

That did nothing to deter the mainlanders who came out by ferry in the warm weather to muck about on the shores of Cutty-hunk, hoping to find what Captain Kidd might have buried or what the currents had stripped from the shipwrecks slowly sur-rendering to rot in the Graveyard.

We liked to watch those mainlanders follow the receding tide out as far as it went, plunging long rods into the sand, hoping for the clunk of metal, sometimes digging up an old lantern or a rusty chain before being chased ashore by the incoming tide.

It never occurred to me, as I watched them search, that I would be the one to find the treasure they sought. Or that I would find it in a place where none of them would ever have dared to look.

Chapter 4

*B*efore Miss Maggie explained why the other islanders were afraid of me, I'd sometimes wondered why people would shake her by the hand but wave at me, instead.

I'd always figured it was because I was little. With a name like Crow. And so different from them, besides, like the calico lobsters that turned up in traps very rarely and always with great to-do.

As I got older, I realized that there was more to it than that.

When I asked Osh about it, he shrugged and talked in circles, as if I'd asked why women don't have beards.

But then, one day, as I came up to the cottage with a pail full of steamers, I overheard him arguing with Miss Maggie and knew it had something to do with me. So I listened, of course.

"It's foolish," he said. "The way they treat her. Like she's made of poison."

"Yes, it is," Miss Maggie said, her voice as sharp as a razor clam. "But it would be better if she understood why, even so."

Osh said, "She's still too young," which sounded odd, coming from the man who had taught me to bait a hook when I was four.

"Well, she's going to have to find out sooner or later."

"Later is fine."

"I don't think so." Miss Maggie sounded like she was digging in her heels. "And I don't like not telling her something she has every right to know."

At which point I ducked through the cottage door and asked them what that "something" was.

Osh wouldn't look at me.

Miss Maggie said, "You shouldn't eavesdrop on other people, Crow."

Osh said, "This is her house, Maggie."

"What do I have every right to know?" I said.

Miss Maggie looked even more serious than usual. "Where you came from," she said.

Which was a very surprising thing for her to say.

"You know where I came from?" I said in a small voice.

"No," Osh said, before Miss Maggie could utter another word. "We don't. You could have come from a hundred places around here. But this is where you came *to*. And this is where you are."

Which didn't explain why the islanders were afraid of me.

"People think I'm made of poison?" I said.

Osh sighed through his teeth. "They don't," he said. "But—"

"Penikese," Miss Maggie blurted. "They think you came from Penikese."

I didn't like the look on Osh's face.

Penikese was a small island a little distance to the west of the other Elizabeths.

Nobody from Cuttyhunk ever went there.

And nobody from Penikese ever came to Cuttyhunk, either.

"It's where sick people used to go," Miss Maggie said. And now she looked too much like Osh did. Part scared. Part sorry we weren't all out digging clams or picking mussels or any of a thousand other things that weren't nearly as hard as this was. "There was a hospital there, Crow. Until a couple of years ago. That's all."

I thought about that. "Was the hospital there when I was a baby?"

Miss Maggie nodded. "Penikese was an island for sick people."

"And I get sick a lot," I said. "Is that why people are afraid of me? Because I get sick a lot?"

Osh nodded. "But that's only because you're small," he said. "I'm sure that's only because you're small. Some people have to work their way through all kinds of sickness before they're strong."

"And I'm one of those people?" I said doubtfully.

Osh bent down to look me straight in the eye. "I'm sure of it," he said.

I turned to Miss Maggie. She hesitated. And then she nodded,

too. "That is true," she said. "Some people start off more suscep-
tible. More . . , vulnerable. Weaker."

"But I'm not," I said. Just the day before, I had helped Osh
carry home a bushel of blue crabs all the way from the toe of
West End Pond.

"No," Osh said. "You're not. Not like you were. Which is
why it's so foolish for people to think you might spread something." I remember how he put his hand on my shoulder. "Unless
it's something good."

But as I lay in bed that night, listening to the sea on the rocks
and the northbound wind, I wondered what kind of sickness
those people had had. The ones on Penikese. The ones who had
been sent to a little island hospital to live far away from everyone
else. Where maybe I myself had been born.

And I didn't want to be from Penikese.

I didn't want to be from a colony of sick people.

I wanted to be from a family with a very good explanation
for why they had sent me to sea in an old boat unlikely to float
for very long.

But I could not think of what that explanation might be, no
matter how hard I tried.

Not long after Miss Maggie told me the truth about Penikese, she
decided it was time for me to go to the little island school with
the few other children on the Elizabeths.

"Why?" Osh said. "She's fine here. She reads all the time, and we're teaching her everything else she needs to know. Leave her be."

"She should be with people her own age," Miss Maggie argued.

"You mean the ones who've never been allowed to play with her?"

"She's fine!" Miss Maggie said. "Anybody can see that just by looking at her."

"They won't see how fine she is," he said. "Or if they do, they'll start to think she should be somewhere better than here, with someone other than me."

At which Miss Maggie had scoffed. "As if there were such a place, or such a person," she said. "As if I would let that happen, regardless."

And she would not let it go.

Until finally he sighed and said, "You'll see," in a voice like November.

So one day that fall, when the sky was the color of forget-me-nots and the sea wanted to play, I reluctantly crossed over to Cuttyhunk with Miss Maggie and followed her up the steps of the schoolhouse, through the door, and straight into the kind of confusion that opened my eyes wide, and then made me want to shut them again, even if I couldn't.

"Look," said a boy near the door, scrambling to his feet. "It's the leper."

I remember looking behind me, to see where "the leper" was, and seeing only Miss Maggie, who grew taller right before my eyes.

"You don't know that," she said to the boy, who had fled to the front of the schoolroom.

The master, Mr. Henderson, came a step closer to us but stopped a fair distance away.

"No, we don't know that," he said. "But we don't know otherwise, neither."

"You're a fool," she said to him in a voice that was equal parts angry and sad.

"Maggie, I'm just trying to keep the other children safe," he said.

"And what if she looked like them? What then?"

He considered me for a long moment. "That has nothing to do with it."

Which added another layer to the confusion that had struck me dumb.

I remember walking back down the steps with Miss Maggie. Looking over my shoulder to see Mr. Henderson wiping the latch with spirits before he closed the door.

"What's a leper?" I said as we turned toward home.

"Someone with leprosy," she said, stomping down the lane toward the bass stands and, beyond them, Osh, waiting for our return. "Which is what those poor people had. The ones who lived on Penikese, in the hospital."

"Is that a bad disease?"

She nodded. "It is."

"And that's what people think I have?"

She stopped suddenly and sat me down in a patch of heather along the lane. "It's very, very unlikely that you have it, Crow, but sometimes a person can have leprosy for years without knowing it."

At which I felt hot and cold at the same time. Too big for my skin. Too small.

"Does that mean I'm going to die?" I sounded like someone else I'd just met for the first time.

"Of course not," she said fiercely. "We don't know that you came from Penikese. And even if you did, you almost certainly do not have leprosy, do you hear me?" She softened a little. "Besides, if you might be a leper, then I might be, too," she said. "And Osh as well."

Which made me feel both better and worse.

"Are people going to be afraid of me forever, then?" I said.

At which Miss Maggie did what she always did when I was worried.

She told me the truth.

"Not forever," she said. "But some people let fear set its hook in them, so it's hard to pull out." She paused. "Leprosy is a terrible disease, Crow. It . . . deforms people. Ruins their bodies. Their skin. Turns their hands into claws."

I looked at my good, fine legs. My smooth skin. My straight fingers.

"And sometimes it damages nerves so badly it's impossible to feel pain." She cleared her throat once. Twice.

"Wouldn't that be a good thing? Not to feel pain?" I said.

But she shook her head. "There's more than one kind of pain," she said. "And if you don't feel it, you can get hurt."

"But it hurts when you do feel it, too," I said.

"Yes," she said, "but feeling hurt and being hurt aren't always the same thing."

Which confused me even more.

So did the idea that I might be a leper.

"But I was just a new baby when I got here," I said. "Osh told me so. Just hours old. How could I have gotten sick so fast?"

Miss Maggie looked me right in the eye. "I am almost completely sure that you are as healthy as a horse, Crow, but I won't lie to you. Leprosy is spread by coughing. Sneezing. Touch. Even tears." She took my hand. "It's not possible to give birth without touch," she said. "Or tears, sometimes."

"But isn't there a cure?" I asked.

Miss Maggie, the best healer on the Elizabeths, the one who always told me the truth, said, "No, I'm afraid not. Though the Bible says Jesus cured lepers."

I thought about that. "Does it say how?"

"Sometimes: miracles," Miss Maggie said. "Sometimes: faith."

Chapter 5

*O*sh didn't say, "I told you so," but he seemed quite pleased when I came home from school so soon after leaving.

"Not much of a school anyway," he said when he heard what had happened.

And he was right.

Sometimes there were only two or three other children on the islands, and Mr. Henderson, the schoolmaster, who was also a ship's pilot, often left them alone while he climbed Lookout Hill to watch for ships that needed guiding through the Graveyard, where hundreds of ships had gone down.

It was hard to imagine that he taught his students anything they couldn't learn on their own.

"You don't need to go to school," Osh told me. "Miss Maggie has already taught you your letters and numbers. If you're hungry enough, you'll learn to fish and farm. The rest is salt and pepper."

But I liked salt and pepper and I wanted to know more than I did.

And I wanted answers to the questions that rose and ebbed and rose again, a tide of curiosity that was as much a part of my life as the sea.

Questions like why I had a spot shaped like a feather on my cheek.

"Because you do," Miss Maggie told me one day as I helped her pull parsnips and carrots from her garden.

When I persisted, she said that some people thought marks like mine were signs of wishes that hadn't come true.

"Whose wishes?" I asked.

"Your mother's," she said gruffly, and then refused to say another word about it.

When I asked her why my hair was curly, she said, "Because it is," and then, when I pressed, she confessed that she didn't know. "Perhaps it runs in your family," she said.

"But Osh doesn't have curly hair," I replied, without thinking first.

And then I realized what I'd said and didn't ask about my hair again.

Mostly, my lessons with Miss Maggie were all business, and she especially had no answer to what I wanted to know most: like why someone had tied me into a leaky skiff and set me adrift on the outgoing tide.

"Can't we find the doctors who ran the hospital on Penikese and ask if I came from there?" I asked her.

She shook her head. "I already wrote to the hospital when you were a baby, but no one ever answered," she said. "I'm sure they would have replied if they'd known anything. And if they knew that someone on Penikese had sent a newborn baby out to sea, don't you think they would have come looking for you?"

To which I had no answer except to ask another question.

"What about the lepers?"

"What about them?"

"Can't we ask them about me?"

"I don't know where they went after Penikese, Crow." She sighed. "Just somewhere south. And besides, if someone sent you away in secret, why would they say so now? And who else would know about it? A real, serious, important secret isn't something you uncover without a lot of digging."

"So let's start digging," I said, though I was more eager now to know where I *hadn't* come from than where I had. If I could prove I wasn't from Penikese, people would have to stop treating me like a leper. Surely, then, they would shake my hand, too.

"Why do you think they left Penikese?" I asked Miss Maggie.

She shrugged. "It's bad enough to be sick. Worse that people don't want to have anything to do with you. Worse still to be locked away on a cold, bare island. I'm sure it was too hard to live out there, for the patients and the doctors, both. It made sense for them to go to a warmer place."

"So I'll never be able to ask them?"

"Ask them what?" she said.

"Whether I came from Penikese?"

"Never's a long time," she said. "Maybe we'll find a way."

When I asked Osh, later that day, he said what he'd always said before: "This is your home. You don't need another one."

"But I don't want another home, Osh. I just want to know where I came from, and whether I might turn into a leper someday."

"And what will that change?" he said. "I won't treat you any different. Miss Maggie won't treat you any different."

"But if it turns out I'm not from Penikese, other people will treat me different," I said, remembering the schoolmaster as he scoured the handle I'd touched. "They'll have to."

Osh was not so sure. "You don't know that," he said.

"But why wouldn't they?"

"Why does anyone do anything?" he said. He sounded tired. "Better to pay attention to your own self, and leave their business to them."

So I tried to do that.

And I was, to my own surprise, largely successful. For a while.

I worked hard to concentrate on what I knew for sure—about Osh and Miss Maggie and me.

I knew that Osh was as much a castaway as I was, though he himself had done the casting. That he could paint a picture that was as real as what was real, only better. That he was stronger than two men. Maybe three. Maybe a thousand.

I knew that Miss Maggie was a castaway, too. Like Osh, by choice. She never said much about why she'd come to Cutty-hunk. Only that she'd been born on a farm, raised on a farm, married to a farmer somewhere far from the sea, and that she had lost it all.

And I knew quite a bit about myself, too, though not everything.

"Nobody knows everything," Osh often said to me. "Especially when they're young."

So I concentrated on that, too: learning what I could about the things right in front of me, like lobstering and shepherding and the constellations riding the night sky.

I hiked up Lookout Hill, where a surfman kept post in a tiny station house, scanning the horizon with a long glass, watching for ships in trouble as they came through the Graveyard, where Vineyard Sound and Buzzards Bay met in a wild and dangerous dance. And I learned a lot about danger that way.

I learned how to pull ticks from Miss Maggie's flock and bathe the sheep in Wash Pond before the shearing. And I learned to shear by practicing on the lambs. Their pink and tender skin taught me how to be more careful than I'd ever been.

I read a dozen new books, like *The Secret Garden* and *The Wonderful Wizard of Oz*—books that rang bells in my heart—and I devoted myself to my lessons with Miss Maggie, who taught me things like why salt water boiled faster than fresh. Why the French had given us the Statue of Liberty. Why Mr. Lincoln's face graced every penny.

And for some time, the sack I carried felt lighter. Sometimes I even forgot that I was carrying it. But it felt, by now, like a part of me, and I found that I couldn't put it aside. Not completely.

Nor did I ever stop watching for signs that I might be on my way to ill.

For a whole year, I didn't see much: a winter cold. Poison ivy when I was careless about where I walked. Garden-variety aches and pains.

But then, shortly after I turned eleven, I was the only one on the islands to come down with influenza.

At least that's what Miss Maggie said it was.

"You shouldn't come near me," I said as I lay in bed, my bones sore, my lips so chapped they bled. "In case it's not the flu."

"Oh, fiddle," Miss Maggie said. "It's flu, plain and simple." And she took my temperature by kissing me lightly on the forehead, as if I were as clean and safe as a teakettle.

But I was sure that neither she nor Osh told anyone else that I was sick again.

And all three of us smiled more than usual on the day when I woke up well.

Chapter 6

*E*verything changed when I had been on the island for twelve years.

I will never forget how small the first step toward that change was. How simple.

The day was fair, the breeze like a song that's easy to remember.

And I was, on that day, in that moment, content to be under the spell of the sea and the islands and the here and now.

Until Miss Maggie said, "I hear there's going to be a bird sanctuary on Penikese soon. They've hired a bird keeper to live over there."

And my world shifted, just a little. In such a small way that I barely noticed.

I was helping her weed her vegetable garden, something we did so often I had begun to think that the weeds were wizards.

She pulled a dandelion just past its bloom, before its seeds could fly.

"A bird keeper on Penikese?" I said. That sounded pretty far-fetched to me. "What kind of keeping do birds need?"

I pictured him making supper for the gulls. Reading them bedtime stories.

Miss Maggie said, "He'll count them, record what kinds there are, whether they're breeding, whether they're sick. That kind of thing."

It sounded like an odd sort of job. Maybe it was done by an odd sort of person.

"He's going to live out there? With the birds?"

"And the rabbits," she said. "That'll be part of his job, too, to make sure there are plenty of rabbits breeding out there."

Now I was sure she was pulling my leg.

"I didn't know rabbits needed help with that."

I thought she might twist my ear, but she surprised me by laughing.

"Nor did I," she said.

"And he's not afraid of getting leprosy?"

Miss Maggie rolled her eyes. "Oh, I'm sure he is. They had to go all the way to Maine before they could find someone willing to take the job. But they sanitized the hospital, and it's been years, for pity's sake."

Not so long before, we'd watched from the top of a drumlin as they'd burned a row of tumbledown sheds. Places not worth sanitizing. Places easier to burn instead.

The flames in the distance, still burning into the night, had made it seem as if the sea itself had caught fire.

I didn't understand how Penikese could suddenly become a bird sanctuary. If it was such a thing, I could not see how it had ever been anything else. Giving it a new name didn't change much.

I wondered what it would be on another day. Who would next need refuge there, and why.

Which gave me something to think about while I helped Miss Maggie pull the rest of the dandelions before they went to seed.

The world shifted again a few weeks later.

Most days, no matter the weather, I climbed to the top of one of the Cuttyhunk drumlins and scanned the mainland across Buzzards Bay, wondering if another person might be standing on another hill over there, looking out toward me, wondering where I was.

The wind, like the sea, was an always kind of thing, but on the hilltops it was even stronger than below, and I felt like a mast as I braced myself up there, my hair like a pennant.

I carried with me a small spyglass I'd found in the sand. It had a little fog inside it and there were barnacle prints glued onto the glass, but I could still see more with it than without.

Most of the time, I climbed in daylight and could see, in the distance, Sow and Pigs Reef where so many ships had foundered, the whirlpools that spun where the currents from east and west met, sometimes the spouts of whales.

On clear, warm nights, especially when the moon showed me the way, I would make the climb in the dark. The lights on the mainland were as familiar to me as the constellations overhead.

Until now I had seen nothing very curious.

But on this particular night, there was another light I'd never seen before.

It was a small yellow light that flickered out in Buzzards Bay, not too terribly far from Cuttyhunk. I could see it better through the glass, but not well enough to know what or where it was exactly.

I decided that it could not be a ship's lantern. I had seen those before. This was bigger and not as steady.

There was no wood on tiny Gull Island, save for a little driftwood, and no people, either.

I thought through the possibilities and decided that it was a fire on Penikese. A small one, in the open, perhaps on the beach.

I heard Miss Maggie coming up behind me. She always made a little puffing sound when she climbed. Like a tiny steam engine.

"Something amiss?" she said when she reached the top.

It didn't surprise me that Miss Maggie was out in the night. She had trouble sleeping, so she walked Cuttyhunk at all hours, visiting her sheep and cattle, which roamed the island freely everywhere except the gated places where most of the people lived.

Miss Maggie and I often crossed paths on moonlit nights and sometimes stopped for a talk or a salt-and-pepper lesson about the stars or the weather.

"There's a fire out there," I said, handing her the spyglass. "On Penikese, I think."

She looked in that direction, put the glass to her eye, and, after a bit, handed it back to me.

"Probably the bird keeper," she said.

"I've never seen a bonfire out there before. Do you think it's a signal?"

"He has a shortwave," she said. "No need for a signal fire."

"But what if his radio's broken and he's out there starving to death?"

"He has a boat," she said.

"But what if that's broken, too?"

Miss Maggie wasn't fond of what-if games, but she humored me this time. "There's plenty to eat out there if he knows anything about the land."

"What, the rabbits? The birds? Wouldn't that be against the rules?"

She shrugged. "I suppose it would." She gave me a hard look. "Why so curious about a fire?"

I didn't have a good answer for that, except: "It's just odd, that's all."

Miss Maggie said, "Well, I know next to nothing about the Penikese bird keeper . . . and I have no idea if that's his fire . . . or if it's even coming from Penikese."

She turned to be on her way.

"Maybe Osh will know," I said.

At which she shook her head. "Have you ever known him to care what happens out there?" she asked.

And she was right.

Osh was not much interested in anything beyond the places where he sailed and walked, none of them as far even as Penikese, which was not so very far from us, after all.

I tried hard to do what Osh wanted—not to care where I'd come from—but I knew more about where he had come from than where I had, and that didn't seem right.

It made me feel too light, as if I were anchored by a different kind of gravity than other people.

Miss Maggie had told me a thing or two about gravity . . . and about how Osh had suddenly appeared in the Elizabeths about a year before I had.

"I saw his sail as he tacked up the coast," she said of the day Osh arrived on our island. "Maybe from Newport or Narragansett or maybe from farther south. And I wondered about it because it was the only blue sail I'd ever seen."

We were putting out seedlings in her kitchen garden, and I nearly planted two tomatoes in the same hole together as she told me the story.

"I walked down to the bass stands and watched as he crossed the bay and sailed straight up to your island without a lick of dithering. Just . . . there he was, pulling his skiff up on the beach below where your cottage is now. And then he threw his things above the wrack line—he didn't have much—and looked around at the rocks and the bit of good land there. Pulled the mast and the sail off the skiff. Flipped the hull upside down. And picked up a big rock and bashed a great hole in the boat."

She lowered a seedling into a hole and gently pressed the earth firm around its slender stem. "I didn't know what to think when he did that. Or when I saw him breaking the hull up for firewood when there's driftwood for that."

She stopped and sat back on her haunches. "First time I'd ever seen a captain wreck his own boat," she said.

I could picture him doing it.

And I wanted to go home right then.

"Why did he do that?" I asked.

Miss Maggie shook her head.

"I didn't know then and I'm still not sure now, but an island is one thing when a man has a boat, quite another when he doesn't."

I tucked that in my pocket to think about later.

"He has a boat now," I said.

"Yes. He has a boat now." She took my chin and leaned down to look into my face, so close that I could see the green in her brown eyes, as if they were little round gardens. "And he has you, too."

Chapter 7

The fire was there again the next night.

This time, I had convinced Osh to come with me to see if it was there.

"Look," I said, pointing out toward Penikese. "Miss Maggie thinks it might be the bird keeper."

Osh shrugged his usual shrug. "Maybe it's more of those foolish people," he said. Sometimes, treasure seekers like the ones we often saw on Cuttyhunk spent time on the islands where no one lived. Other times, rich people sailed up from Newport to Gull Island, which was right alongside Penikese, to camp out in the "wilderness" for a night or two.

I liked to sleep out, too, when the weather was fair, the sky sagging with stars. But those rich people slept in tents or staterooms that had no stars. If they'd really wanted wilderness, there was plenty of it on the mainland, complete with bears and coyotes and mosquitoes. Gull Island had fiddler crabs and piping plovers.

I knew why Osh thought they were foolish.

Miss Maggie had told me how he started his island life with nothing except that blue sail for shelter, even in a storm, and nothing much to eat but starfish soup in those first few days after he stranded himself there.

"Starfish soup?" It was hard to imagine anyone being hungry enough to eat starfish.

"He had trouble catching fish from the shore, especially without the right kind of gear. Wherever he had fished before, it wasn't anywhere like here," she said. "I spent some time watching him, wondering why he didn't come over to Cuttyhunk to fish off the bass stands. After another day or two, I saw him pulling starfish off the rocks at low tide."

I told her that I had never heard of starfish soup.

She laughed her tight little laugh. "He, Daniel . . . Osh . . . didn't talk back then. Not one bit, though I called to him across the sand a few times, hoping he'd answer. And some of the men around here gave him trouble about squatting on their fishing ground, but he never even looked at them, let alone answered. So I didn't know until much later what he did with those starfish." She was still smiling at the thought. "When I finally knew him well enough to ask, he told me he had taken just one leg from each of them, to flavor the rainwater he cooked on his fire.

'Better to have only four legs than to be dead,' he said. 'Better to eat starfish soup than starve.'"

I imagined the rocks covered with lopsided starfish. And Osh, that hungry.

"When did he start to talk?"

"After you came along," she said.

———

Osh and I stood on the hill, looking out at the fire in the distance.

"I'd like to sail over and find out whose fire that is," I said. "I looked over this morning and I don't think it's campers up from Newport. I didn't see a pleasure boat."

He snorted. "Well, if you didn't see one, one must not exist."

He looked, in the moonlight, much younger than he was.

"Why didn't you talk when you first got here?" I asked.

I expected him to be startled by such an out-of-the-blue question, but Osh wasn't startled by much.

Still, he took his time before he said, "What does that have to do with a strange fire?"

"Nothing, I guess. Except that the fire you made when you first came here must have looked strange to someone across the water. And maybe they thought *you* were a foolish person from Newport, instead of a man eating starfish soup."

When Osh didn't want to talk, he didn't, so I was surprised when he answered me.

"I didn't talk because I had nothing to say. And there was no one to listen."

"There was Miss Maggie."

"Yes, there was Miss Maggie. A woman with a voice like a warden, barking at me from the bass stands. She started calling me Daniel because she felt bad yelling across at me without a proper name. Tried calling across in French, a little, and some Spanish, in case one of those was my language." He shook his head. "The woman was determined."

"But you talked to her eventually." I had wrapped this thread around my finger and was pulling on it as gently as I could, lest it break. Osh had never told me anything much about that time, before me.

"Not for a long while, I didn't. But when you arrived, and she heard you crying, she came all the way across, right up to my door, with a bottle of cow's milk so fresh it was still warm and a flour sack she'd made into bunting for you to sleep in."

I waited.

"And then she came over again and again, always with something new in her basket."

"Like what?"

"Like oat mash and a salt spoon to feed you with when milk wasn't enough. A little brandy when you started teething, which I made her take away right then." He kept his eyes on the distant fire. "Babies cry when they hurt. Didn't bother me."

"But maybe it bothered me."

He shook his head. "Not enough for brandy," he said.

I waited some more. "What else?"

"Oh, clover honey when you were old enough for it. Clothes. A pair of little boots brought over on the ferry. Things like that."

"Didn't she ever bring anything for you?"

He turned and started back down the hill. "Made me that sweater I have. Sheared the wool, dyed it with indigo, spun it, knitted it, too big. Brought it over with a kettle of chowder and told me to grow into it."

I smiled. Miss Maggie was as skinny as a spring goat, but she didn't like to see anyone else too thin.

I followed him down the path. "So, do you think the fire is on Penikese?" I asked.

"I suppose it is," he said. "But a fire's a fire. Nothing so odd about that. It's just the bird keeper. Or a camper. Or another idiot treasure hunter. Why do you care?"

"Because I do," I said. "Because all of a sudden someone is building bonfires out there. There has to be a reason."

"There's always a reason," Osh said. "But what does that have to do with you?"

"Maybe nothing," I admitted. "I just want to go over and look around. Everyone thinks I was born there. But nobody *knows* that. I want to know, Osh. And maybe the bird keeper can tell me something about who used to live there. And whether there was ever a baby."

Osh walked ahead of me, a little faster than before. I almost did not hear him when he said, "You start looking back now and you might not see where you're going."

This from a man who knew exactly where he'd been born and when and to whom.

I hurried up to walk alongside him. "Will you take me out there tomorrow for a look?"

Osh shook his head. "I will not," he said. "It's warm enough to put out the seedlings. You'll help me with that tomorrow."

"The next day, then?"

But Osh did not answer me.

And it was at that moment that I began to plan my trip to Penikese, with him or without.

Osh was even more quiet than usual as we put out the seedlings the next day.

The sun on my back was nice. The soft dirt was warm, too. But the memory of the fire on Penikese was warmer than anything, and I had trouble keeping my mind on my work.

"You just planted two peppers together," Osh said. "Which means two little plants instead of two big ones."

"At least they won't be lonely," I said. But Osh didn't laugh.

I eased the shoots out of the earth and gently combed their roots apart.

"Sorry," I said to the peppers, which seemed content to have been twined.

Osh didn't say anything else all morning, but when he

brought bowls of mutton stew to the garden for our lunch, he said, "Tomorrow we can go out there."

I was surprised at two things: one, that he would take me there; two, that I felt a little sorry because I wouldn't be going alone.

I didn't want to feel . . . apologetic about this trip to Penikese. Or to stand in the shadow of Osh's impatience, his suspicion that this was a wild-goose chase.

But I was also relieved at the prospect of Osh in my boat. He might not like the idea that I had a root in soil we didn't share, but he was never mean. And I trusted him.

"We'll ask Miss Maggie if she'd like to come, too," he said, which was the third and biggest surprise. Osh seemed to like Miss Maggie's company, but he had never sought it unless I was sick.

"Why?" I asked.

Osh ate his stew, looking steadily into the bowl as if it knew the answer better than he did.

"She'll bring a picnic," he said.

A good enough reason but not the real one, which he soon gave me.

"And she can talk to that birdman if he's there."

That made more sense. Osh would not need to talk to anyone if Miss Maggie came along.

"I can talk to the bird keeper," I said.

"You're too small," Osh said. "He'll talk to me before he'll talk to you. And he'll talk to Miss Maggie before he'll talk to either of us."

I nodded, not happy at such an idea, but glad that Miss Maggie might be going with us.

"I'll ask her after supper," I said.

And of course she said yes. No one liked an adventure more than Miss Maggie. As long as she could come home again afterward.

Chapter 8

*T*hat night, as I climbed into bed, Osh surprised me yet again by handing me a small wooden box that had once held spice from the mainland. It still smelled like cinnamon when I opened it.

Inside there was a piece of paper, folded twice.

"What's this?"

He tipped his head. "Look."

The paper was old and tattered. Osh sat beside me and held his lantern closer.

Osh could tell good stories when he wanted to, but he couldn't read at all. "Do you know what this says?" I asked.

He shook his head.

I peered at the paper. The words on it were faded, some beyond reading, and in places the paper was so damaged that the writing had rubbed away. There wasn't much left. Just little islands of words. I read them aloud, for both of us.

if I could

for now

    hope you

bright sea

                    better off

lambs   *little feather*

    I left something

            day it might help

"What is this?" I asked again.

Osh didn't look at me. "When I found you and peeled away the cloth you were wrapped in, I discovered this pressed against your chest. It was wet, and some of the ink had run, and it came away from your skin in pieces." He didn't sound like the Osh I knew. "I laid it flat and put it back together and dried it. For you. For now."

I looked again at the letter. At the handwriting. For all the damage to the paper, the writing still looked like a woman's, I thought. *My mother's,* I thought.

It was the first time I really believed I had a mother, though I knew I had not sprung up out of nothing. It just felt that way.

"I don't know what it means," I said.

"I don't, either," Osh said. "I didn't think there was enough of it left to make any sense."

"But what if it did?" I said. "Why didn't you tell me about this before?"

Osh bowed his head. His hands, resting in his lap, were covered with scars from all his work and whatever had happened before me.

"When you first came here, I didn't think I'd get to keep you," he said. "If people hadn't been so afraid that you were from Penikese, they would have taken you away for sure."

I tried to picture that: Osh bolting the door. Locking the windows. Hiding me under the bed.

"Miss Maggie wasn't afraid," I said, "and she didn't try to take me."

Osh nodded. "Miss Maggie isn't like other people."

I guess I understood all that, but I still didn't understand why he had waited so long to show me what was in the spice box, and I said as much.

"I always meant to show you," he said. "When you were old enough."

But I'd been old enough for some time now. "You know how much I've wanted to find out where I came from," I said.

He sighed. Ran his hands through his hair. "And then? If you found out where you came from?"

"Then I'd know," I said, baffled by how upset he was. "Why would that be such a bad thing?"

"You're still a young girl," he said. "Not too old to be taken away." He looked at his hands. "Or to go because you wanted to be somewhere better than a shack on a rock in the middle of nowhere."

It was hard for me to believe that this man, who was as strong as February and August combined—and smart, besides—would be afraid of something like that.

I leaned my head against his arm. "I'm happy here with you," I said. "I won't be any less happy if I know where I came from. And I won't want to go back there. Especially if I'm from Penikese." I closed my eyes. "I want to know, that's all."

I felt Osh sigh.

"Some folks might not give you the choice," he said. "Your people might want you back."

I smiled, knowing he couldn't see my face. "First off, if they had wanted me they wouldn't have sent me away, especially not like they did." I handed the paper back and scuttled under my blanket. "Second, you are my people."

He looked at me, the lantern light golden on his eyes. "I came here to be by myself. But the thought of being here alone now? Without you?" He cleared his throat. "I can't think that thought. It won't stay long enough to make sense."

I reached up and tugged on his ear. "Good," I said. "Then let it fly away."

I closed my eyes.

"There was something else with the letter," he said.

I opened my eyes again. "What?"

He held out the spice box again.

I sat up and found, in the bottom of the box, a scrap of rough cloth tied into a bundle with some twine.

"Did you open it?" I asked. It weighed almost nothing.

"Yes."

I pulled on the twine and found a ring nestled in the fold of cloth. I held it up in the light and was surprised to see the gleam of a red gemstone.

It was too big, even for my biggest finger.

"Do you think I'm from Newport, then?" I whispered. *"From a rich family?"*

Osh shook his head. "Everything else about you said *poor*."

"Then where did this come from?"

He shrugged. "It's real gold. That's all I know."

"How can you tell?"

"It's very old," he said, "and there's dirt in where the ruby sits, but the gold hasn't gone green like buried brass would have. Or bronze."

I could not stop looking at the ring. I could not stop thinking about who had worn it last.

I put it back and set the box on the windowsill by my bed. "Will you help me figure out what it means?"

He sighed. "We're going to Penikese tomorrow, aren't we?"

I kissed his cheek. "We are," I said. "Good night."

He said some words in his other language. And then he went

out into the night, calling, "Mouse!" in a voice that was hoarse for no good reason.

I closed my eyes and saw, in my own darkness, the letter someone had laid on my chest. That handwriting. That pale ink. The blank spaces in between.

And I dreamed again about the sea and whales nearby and a dark, rocking world full of stars.

Chapter 9

The next day was bright and breezy. Perfect for a sail.

The tide was inbound, the wind out of the east, which made it easy for us to reach Copicut Neck where Miss Maggie was waiting for us with a hamper of lunch.

"Go on home," she told her mare, Cinders, who was so gentle and smart that Miss Maggie could ride bareback and then turn her loose to meander home.

"You take the food," she said when I offered to help her aboard the skiff. "The day I need help into a boat from a sprout like you is the day I stay onshore with the widows and babies."

"Yes, ma'am," I said, climbing in after her.

I wanted badly to tell her about the letter and the ring, but not now, not here, and not when Osh was with us. I knew Miss Maggie would have questions, but Osh had been especially quiet all morning. I didn't think he'd feel like giving her any answers.

Instead, he sat in the stern, his hand on the tiller, while Miss Maggie and I perched across from each other, ducking under the boom when Osh came about, otherwise enjoying the wind and the spray.

A pair of dolphins traveled along with us for a bit, sleek and smiling, and I didn't think I'd ever seen anything as beautiful.

Not so long before, the lighthouse keeper on Cuttyhunk had used dolphin fat to fuel his beacon, and I could not remember that without shrinking.

When this pair cut away for open water, they leaped in tandem, again and again, like colts in a blue meadow.

Penikese looked small at first, not much bigger up close. The near shore, all rocks below a bluff, gave us no good place to land, so we sailed around to the harbor where it was easier.

Along that coast there was a skiff tied up at a pier and the remnants of ruined buildings—cellar holes and such—and when we climbed up from the beach we could see knee-high stone walls that straggled across the moors like old scars. Rabbit trails. A dirt lane that seemed to lead nowhere. But no sign of the bird keeper.

"Probably off somewhere making sure the rabbits are making more rabbits," I said.

Which drew a puzzled look from Osh, a laugh from Miss Maggie.

"Never mind about the rabbits," she said. "His boat is here, so he is, too. We'll see him soon enough. Nowhere much to go on this island except round and round."

She was right. From where we stood, we could see most of

the island except where it dipped into swales or hid behind low hills and boulders.

"They lived on the other side of the island," Miss Maggie said. "On the other side of that hill," which rose up as if even the island itself had meant to keep the sick in their own, lonely place.

I felt twice as heavy as I had moments before. But I picked up one foot and then the other and led the way in that direction along the remnants of the old lane where pasture grass now struggled to grow.

There wasn't a single living tree on the island, just cedar skeletons and patches of green-gray shrubs. Mostly, the island was a hilly moor of sharp grass and wildflowers stretching from shore to shore like a lumpy quilt.

"Woadwaxen," Osh suddenly said, coming to a stop.

It sounded like neither English nor his other, private tongue. But I knew it to be part of his third language—the one he used when making paints.

"For yellow," he said, pointing.

This was something we did together, on Cuttyhunk and the other islands where we sailed sometimes in search of petals we could boil into dyes and mix into paints. He had taught me which plants made which colors and how to mix them to make more, and I loved being his assistant in both the kitchen and the field. He would utter something simple, like "aster," or something odd, like "Calopogon," and I would go, much like a setter after a duck, to fetch it for his basket.

I did that now, cutting off the lane to gather some woadwaxen for his yellow. It was a tough thing that didn't want to go with me, but I pinched off a number of new blooms and tucked them in my pockets. They wouldn't yield much, but sometimes Osh painted a single yellow flower in a pale green marsh, and it was all the better for being just one.

I stayed in the rough, walking parallel to the road for a bit, in hopes of finding a teaberry to chew on. Instead, I found myself hobbled by a soft spot that buried my right foot. Had I been running, I would have been hurt.

Miss Maggie came to help me up. "Maybe an old stump well," she said.

"If it is, where's the tree that lived here?"

"Gone to a fire, I suppose." She looked about. "See there? All that old wood in the heather? The last of what grew here. This island was all trees, once."

I could see other sandy spots ahead where nothing grew. When I tested them, the ground was soft there, too. I imagined the cedars that were now cut and dried and split into house shingles.

"Odd that the holes are still soft after all this time," I said.

Miss Maggie frowned. "Sand will do that to the ground," she said, though dubiously.

Osh had gone ahead without us along the road, and we hurried to catch up.

"Pimpernel," he said, pointing. And again I left the lane to fill my pockets, more careful now about where I stepped.

When we reached the top of the highest hill, we found a brick reservoir and a big curved boulder where we sat to rest.

From there, we could see a couple of kettle ponds in the distance and a row of buildings on a wind-scoured bluff overlooking Buzzards Bay. In the middle, a big structure. On either side, plain cottages facing the water.

"That's where they lived," Miss Maggie said quietly, and we soon headed down the hill toward them.

As we approached the cottages, we found the remnants of a garden, but everything in it had gone wild. A thatch of blackberry bushes. And mounds of earth, as if someone had been digging for potatoes or carrots, though I didn't see anything like that growing here. And a bit farther along, at the end of the row of cottages, a black spot on the ground where a fire had been, some bones in the ash, some feathers, the gleam of grease. A cooking fire, I thought. Someone had cooked a bird here. And I had seen his fire.

"This is the leprosarium," Miss Maggie said as she led us to the steps of the big building among the cottages. "The hospital where they treated the lepers."

Osh and I stood and stared. "I wonder how many lepers lived here."

"Not so many," Miss Maggie said.

"How do you know?"

She looked a little abashed. "I went to the library."

She knew how I felt about the library and she shared my displeasure. Years earlier, when they first discovered that she was borrowing books for our lessons, they gave her the books outright rather than put them back on their shelves . . . and they told her that she could no longer check out books if they were meant for my hands.

Of course she continued to take out books, without telling the librarian that they were meant for me, and I was tempted to kiss every page of them for good measure before she returned them. "What nonsense," she said again and again. "What utter hogwash."

But the library had a good collection for such a small town, and I was not sorry that Miss Maggie had gone looking.

"Most of the lepers came to America already sick," she said. "From Russia, some of them. Japan. Turkey. Tobago. China. And Cape Verde. Other places."

I knew about Cape Cod. It was our mainland to the north. But I had never heard of Cape Verde.

I turned to her. "Where's Cape Verde?" I asked.

She looked steadily at the hospital. "Islands off Senegal."

"Where's Senegal?"

"Africa," she said.

"What about Tobago?"

"Another island. Off the coast of Venezuela."

"Where's Venezuela?"

"Oh, for goodness' sake, Crow, we'll have a geography lesson when we get home," she said.

"Where's Venezuela?" I repeated.

"South America."

I looked at my arms. They were the same color Osh made by mixing purple and yellow, blue and orange, red and green.

I wondered what people on those other islands looked like.

Maybe I was a real islander after all. Just not an Elizabeth Islander. Except I was here, on the Elizabeths, regardless of where else I might belong.

"Lots of people come here from other places, right?" I said.

"What, here? Penikese? I just told you they did, Crow."

"I didn't mean just here," I said.

Osh started up the stairs.

"Should we really go in there?" Miss Maggie asked.

Osh kept on. "Why did we come here if not to go in?"

But Miss Maggie and I waited where we were while Osh crossed the porch and knocked on the door.

No one answered, even when Osh knocked again, harder.

He tried the door but it was locked. "Who locks his door when he's the only one living on an island?" He peered through a porch window alongside the door and then returned to the yard, shrugging.

"Maybe he didn't hear you," I said, climbing the porch steps.

"No one's there, Crow," Miss Maggie said.

But I knocked hard, regardless. And that was when I heard a thump inside. A heavy noise from above, I thought, like something had fallen.

I raised my fist to knock again but just then, from around the line of cottages, came a man.

He was carrying a shovel in one hand, a long gun in the other.

Chapter 10

*T*he man stopped dead at the sight of us, his gun coming up and then, just as quickly, sagging again.

We must have presented an odd picture: big Osh, Miss Maggie, and me.

"What are you all doing there?" he said loudly, coming forward quickly now. He talked with an accent I didn't know. Not a foreigner, exactly, but not from around here, either.

He was a big man, bigger even than Osh, with a square head and a flat, ruddy face. Neither young nor old, dressed in land colors, head to toe.

"What do you want?" he said.

"I'm Maggie, this is Daniel, and this is Crow," Miss Maggie said, smiling hard as I joined them. "We were out sailing, from Cuttyhunk, and thought we'd have a look around. You don't mind, do you?"

The keeper did not return her smile. "I certainly do, and so do the birds," he said. "And I'd rather they didn't." He glanced up at the hospital and suddenly turned away, talking as he walked. "Come see here," he said, beckoning.

We followed him to the edge of the bluff above the rocky beach.

"Cormorants," he said, pointing toward the big black birds perched on the rocks below. "Herring gulls. Terns. Pipers. Plovers. Yellowlegs. I'm the custodian. The gamekeeper. No hunting allowed here."

"Do we look like hunters?" Miss Maggie asked.

"There are all kinds of hunters," he said.

"Why do you have a gun, then," I asked, "if there's no hunting here?"

"Big gulls eat the eggs of little gulls," he said. "Too many geese and I thin out the flock."

"And roast them?" I asked, remembering the fire.

He didn't answer.

"And why do you have a shovel?" I asked.

He frowned. "They should have named you Badger," he said.

Osh said, "Hey," and took a step toward the man, at which Miss Maggie grabbed him by the arm, me by the hand, and said, "Well, if you don't mind us having a walk around, we'll be very careful not to disturb the birds."

The bird keeper shook his head. "Plover eggs in the sand look like stones," he said. "Too late, after you've already stepped on one."

Miss Maggie nodded. "Yes, but no good mother will let us near her eggs."

And the words were out of my mouth before I felt them coming: "Was there ever a baby here?"

Miss Maggie squeezed my hand.

The bird keeper glared at me. "A baby what?"

"A baby. A baby person. When there were lepers here."

He took a step back, which made no sense.

"I have nothin' to do with that," he said too loudly. "They've been gone for years and soon everything they left behind will be burned. Should burn the graveyard, too, if you ask me, if dirt and bones would burn."

And I was the one now, who stepped back and then, turning, walked a bit away.

Osh followed.

Miss Maggie said, "We'll be careful of the birds."

"See that you do," he said, climbing the hospital steps. "And don't go poking about where y'all don't belong. I'll expect you off this island in short order. And with nothing but what you had when you come."

I thought of the flowers plumping out my pockets and was glad they couldn't speak, but I didn't imagine they would sell me down the river even if they could. Not to this man.

He unlocked the door and turned, looking both nervous and mean, which was odd, I thought. "This here is state land, you know. Not a playground."

He went through and shut the door too hard.

I heard him lock it.

And that was that.

"What a cold man," Miss Maggie said.

"Hiding something," Osh said.

"He talked funny," I said.

"Not funny," Miss Maggie said thoughtfully. "He's from somewhere south."

"I thought you said he was from Maine?"

She nodded. "I thought he was. I guess not."

I turned toward the nearest cottage. "I want a look inside there," I said. But as I turned to glance back at the hospital, I saw the bird keeper watching us from the window. "Maybe let's walk a while first, though."

Across the island we went, single file, along a trail that meandered over the rolling moor, through the beach plum and sea heather, toward the northernmost point of the island.

Along here, again, were bare spots in the ground cover. Just random things. I pointed them out.

"The man carries a shovel," Osh said. "He's digging for something."

"Or burying," Miss Maggie said. "Maybe carrion. So the buzzards don't come."

"What's carrion?" I asked.

"Dead animals. Dead anything."

"Must be a lot of dead anything on this island," I said.

And we were upon the leper graveyard before we knew it.

Around the edge was a picket fence.

We opened the gate and went quietly in among the little headstones and metal medallions, all in rows.

To one side there was a wooden marker with a lamb carved on it and a single word: MORGAN.

"Is a lamb buried here?" I asked.

Miss Maggie came closer. When I looked up at her, I found her eyes not on the marker but on me.

"That means there's a baby buried here," she said. "Named Morgan. But that can't be."

I knelt down and ran my fingers over the carving. "Why not?"

"There was a baby born here right after the colony started, but they sent him off to the mainland, to an orphanage. He would be a man by now."

"How do you know that?"

"The library had some notes the doctor published. Dr. Eastman. They said nothing about another baby. Just that one little boy, who didn't die on Penikese."

"Then what baby is buried here?" I asked.

She shook her head. "I don't know," she said.

I climbed to my feet and brushed the dead grass off my knees.

"Can we find out?" I asked.

"Crow, it's clearly not you buried there. Why do you want to know?"

"Can we find out?" I asked again.

Miss Maggie sighed. "I suppose we can try," she said.

Osh didn't say a thing. He stared at the lamb on the marker, at me, at the sea. And when he turned to leave the graveyard, we followed.

We cut across the island to get back to the harbor, twisting and turning down the rabbit trails, until we reached the bluff overlooking the dock where we'd landed.

From there, I could see a long line of bare spots all along the edge of the bluff. They looked like big round footprints, as if a giant horse had galloped along there.

"Look," I said, pointing.

"More and more," Miss Maggie said. "Curiouser and curiouser."

Osh said, "Digging, not burying."

"But what's he digging for?" Miss Maggie said. "Too dry there for clams."

"Same thing all the other fools dig for," Osh said.

I knew what he meant: the mainlanders with their rods and shovels, hoping for pirate gold or shipwreck treasure.

"Hmm," Miss Maggie mused. "He didn't strike me as a fool on a lark."

"Mean," Osh said. "And nervous to have us here."

I remembered the thump I'd heard inside the hospital just before the bird keeper came around the corner with his gun. I couldn't imagine what had made that sound, but I agreed with Osh: The man had seemed nervous.

"And eager to have us go," Miss Maggie said.

I pictured the bird keeper digging up the whole island, one plug at a time, while the terns and the plovers swooped around his head, fearful for their eggs.

And I thought of the ruby ring in the cinnamon box on my windowsill.

"He must have reason to think there's something here," Osh said.

"Or just bored to tears," Miss Maggie said. "The wind alone would drive some people mad."

"I don't think he's that kind of mad," I said. "I think he's the angry kind of mad."

"He hasn't found what he's looking for," Osh said. "And he's not here for the birds."

At which Miss Maggie continued on toward the skiff. "We'll have our picnic and we'll go," she said. "And when we're home we'll do some digging of our own."

"I wanted to see the cottages," I said.

"Some other day," she replied. "We'll come back soon. Won't we Osh?"

To which he did not reply.

I was tempted to let the whole thing go after that.

Maybe Miss Maggie was right and I wasn't a leper, whether I'd come from Penikese or not. So why worry about it?

Maybe Osh was right: Even if I proved I wasn't from Penikese, the other islanders might still treat me like I was a frightening oddity—for any number of reasons. Or none at all.

But maybe my heart was right when it recognized that sad island. Those weary old cottages. That little graveyard with its picket fence and its headstones and its lamb. And, most of all, that frayed and tattered letter stuck to my chest like a scar.

They were connected.

I thought maybe they were connected.

But I didn't know how.

Chapter 11

I had never written to anyone before and I wasn't the one holding the pen now, but Miss Maggie told me that this was my letter to compose.

"How will we know where to send it?" I asked.

"That book in the library. By Dr. Eastman. He wrote it in Louisiana. Carville, Louisiana. How many leper colonies can there be in just one town?" she said. "This will find him, all right."

The letter was mostly questions, which I asked while walking in circles around Miss Maggie's kitchen table as she sat there, writing them down. I felt about ten feet tall.

Mouse had followed me to Miss Maggie's and she now shadowed me as I walked my laps, which made me feel taller still.

These were my questions:

What was the first baby's name? The one born right after the colony opened?

Where did they send him?

Who was his mother? Who was his father?

Was there another baby named Morgan who is now buried on Penikese?

By the same mother?

How did Morgan die?

Was there yet another baby that was sent away in a skiff?

Miss Maggie paused at this one. "If the doctor knew about such a thing, you can be sure he would have come looking for you," she said.

"You told me he never answered your letter," I said. "When I was a baby and you wanted to know where I had come from."

"That's true, he didn't," she said.

"But maybe he'll answer you now."

So she wrote down my last question, too, with a sigh. "I can just imagine him reading this and wondering why we're asking such things," she said.

I read back over the questions she'd written down and added two more. "Is the mother still alive? Is the father?"

My voice squeaked a little. Mouse gave me an odd look. She rubbed her jaw against my leg.

Miss Maggie got up from the table and fetched a slice of bacon for Mouse—who threw it into the air and wrestled it to the ground before dragging it out into the sunshine—and a ginger snap for me.

We sat quietly while I ate the snap as slowly as possible and let my thoughts settle.

There were so many possibilities. I might have a mother. And a father. And a brother. Or only two of these. Or one. Or none. And no way to know where to look next. Or whether to look at all.

The whole thing made my head hurt.

"I can't think of any more questions right now," I said. "Nothing that the doctor can answer."

"Nor can I," she said, handing me the pen. "Sign at the bottom."

I took the pen.

"What do I write?" I asked.

"Your name," she said with a laugh.

"What, just *Crow*?"

"Yes," she said. "Crow."

"And nothing else?"

She shrugged. "What else is there?"

But that was one of the things that might come back by return post. Another name. And suddenly I wasn't sure I wanted to dig any deeper than I already had.

I spent the next week working hard. While Osh and I tended our garden, I imagined the letter riding the ferry to New Bedford. I pictured it on a truck bound for Boston while we mended our nets and chinked holes where winter had come through our walls. I had a harder time imagining the airplane that flew it south. I'd seen one or two high up over the islands and knew what they were, but I failed to understand how all that heavy machinery did not plunge to the ground, my little letter with it. After the first week, I began to go down to the ferry dock to wait for the mail each morning.

I must have looked so hopeful and eager that the postmaster, Mr. Johnson, acted less cranky with me than he usually did. When he came down to the dock to collect the daily mail from the ferry, he said, with a brisk nod, "I will see it gets to you straightaway when it comes, and no delay whatsoever." But he kept his distance when he said it.

And though I believed that he would deliver the letter when it came, I still sat on the rocks each day and watched the ferry come in, hoping it had brought me a reply.

Hoping, too, that it hadn't.

Osh shook his head over the whole business. "What you do is who you are," he said.

I knew he was right but I asked him, anyway, "And what if you were one thing and became another?"

He nodded. "I was," he said. "I did."

"So?"

"So that's writ in stone. The rest in water."

He was sitting in the shade of the house, painting a picture of storm clouds and a small boat beneath.

I teased Mouse down to the beach with a string and watched her chase it in circles until she keeled over.

"Silly cat," I said as she came to her senses and rolled in the dry sand.

"If you've nothing to do," Osh called, "you could gather some driftwood."

That, and many other chores besides. The birds kept planting weeds in our garden, Miss Maggie wanted fresh straw in her rabbit hutch, and I had yet to pick the blue mussels that we'd be steaming for our supper.

As if he'd read my mind, Osh called, "Bring the mussels up in plenty of brine, and pull some spring onions, too."

But the ferry would be in soon, and I figured I'd start with that.

The tide was mid-high, so I waded through the fast current and came out soaked on the other side, my clothes dripping nicely to cool the warm day. After every wet crossing, I would shake like a dog and wring out my clothes as best I could so they dried in ridges white with salt.

I didn't care.

Osh didn't care.

We were sea clean and sun dried, the two of us, and fine that way.

Miss Maggie didn't approve. She made her own soap and insisted on giving me a bar from time to time, "to take the itch out."

She was right—the sea did leave an itch when it dried—but the soap made me smell sweeter than I was. And Mouse liked me better salty.

"No letter for you, I'm afraid," Mr. Johnson said as he came down the dock, the mailbag slung over one shoulder. "Maybe tomorrow."

He made a detour around me and continued past.

"Well, if it does come and I'm not here, where will you take it?" Which brought him up short.

"If it's addressed to you, it's yours," he said slowly. "But you have no proper address, Crow. I'll give it to Miss Maggie. She can give it to you."

And that's what he did.

Sometimes, when there was a need, another ferry came in the afternoon, and on that day a second one did, bringing another bag of mail with a single letter in it: for me.

"Crow!" Miss Maggie called from atop a bass stand across from our island while I picked mussels off the rocks below.

"I'm down here!" I called back. "I'm coming around."

I clambered over the rocks to where I could see her and she me.

"Your letter," she said, holding it aloft.

I stood up straight.

"Did you open it?"

"Of course not!"

"Will you?"

"Of course not!" she said again, and headed back across the planks to firm ground while I went up to meet her, my pail of mussels sloshing as I went.

I sat next to her on a flat rock in the sun, far enough away so my wet clothes didn't weep onto hers. She held out the envelope.

I could see that it said *Crow* and *Cuttyhunk Island, Massachusetts,* on it. And three pretty stamps. Red and blue stripes, and purple circles with numbers in them.

I didn't care if I ever got another letter: This one would be enough.

"Go ahead," I said. "My hands are wet. You go ahead."

Across the channel I could see Osh in the garden, pulling weeds.

I kept my eyes on him as she opened the envelope and unfolded the letter inside.

Chapter 12

"*D*ear Crow," Miss Maggie read.

> *Thank you very much for your letter. I have wondered, since leaving Penikese, whether there might be people like you who are curious not about the disease itself but rather about the people I treated. Often, I am asked to be a doctor and to speak as one. Rarely am I asked for the stories of the people who spent the last of their lives with me on that island, and of the people who came with me when we left.*
>
> *Your questions concern both those who stayed behind and one nurse who made that long journey to this new home in the south.*
>
> *I will answer them as best I can.*
>
> *To start with:* What was the first baby's name? The one born right after the colony opened?

Unlike some of your questions, these are ones I can answer, but perhaps not to your satisfaction. The baby was born Jason Dias. He was a healthy boy, but his mother, Susanna, was not. Nor, I fear, was his father, Elvan, both of whom died on that island. What Jason is called now, I do not know. He was sent to an orphanage in New Bedford as soon as he was born, before his parents ever even held him, after which I had cause to visit him only three times: once each year until he was three. He showed no signs of disease, so I did not visit him again after that. And I never heard whether he became sick or was ever adopted. Healthy or not, he came from a place that caused most people to treat him poorly. But if he was adopted, he might well have a different name now than the one his mother gave him.

It pained me to have to tell her that he was at the orphanage still and growing up away from the other children, away from everyone, really, and would not talk at all. I tried to lie to her after I first visited the orphanage, but I am a poor liar, and she was very smart. She knew that life would not be easy for her son. But to know that he was never rocked to sleep or cradled in a woman's arms was like poison to her, and I confess that it was a relief when I no longer had to tell her such things.

Miss Maggie looked up and sighed.

"What about the other baby," I said. "What about Morgan?"

At which Miss Maggie resumed her reading, though she sounded weary with it.

> *The story of the baby Morgan is an odd one,* she read.
> *Yes, the same mother, Susanna, did carry another child,*
> *several years after Jason was born, but she was living in one*
> *of the little cottages and took care of herself quite well at*
> *the time, with her husband and my nurse, Miss Evelyn, to*
> *help her. It was only after the baby was born that I learned*
> *of the birth. It happened in the night, and by morning*
> *they had buried the child and would not speak of it except*
> *to say it had been stillborn but otherwise perfect, as far as*
> *they could tell. I could never understand why they had not*
> *come for me when the labor began or why they buried the*
> *baby so quickly, without a minister even. But grief has its*
> *own reasons. And theirs was profound.*
> *Still, they said that perhaps Morgan was better off*
> *with God than alone in this world.*

Again, Miss Maggie stopped reading. She looked into the distance without speaking for a while and then continued on.

> *After that, Susanna began to fail rapidly and died*
> *within a few months. She is buried on Penikese, her*
> *husband with her, though he lingered for another year after*
> *she passed.*

There is, he wrote, *one other person who has something to say about these things. The nurse. Miss Evelyn Morgan. She was on Penikese with us before coming along to Louisiana. She and Susanna were close friends. So close that Susanna chose the name* Morgan *for her second child. To honor her friend. More a sister, really.*

Miss Evelyn was very excited to know that you were asking about Susanna.

I cannot tell you anything about a third child being sent away in a skiff (what a very unusual thing to ask). There was no third child, of that I am quite certain. But Miss Evelyn was anxious that you should write to her. Perhaps, she said, there is something else she can tell you to assuage your curiosity.

Mine, in fact, has been aroused not only by your questions but by your reasons for posing them.

If you feel inclined to share that information, please write again.

Until then, I remain,

And here he signed his name with a great flourish, and *the 8th of June, 1925,* and *Carville, Louisiana.*

"So," Miss Maggie said, the letter still in her hand, her hand in her lap. "There was no third baby, Crow. Just Jason, who was sent away. And Morgan, who died at birth. You are not from Penikese."

I felt surprisingly, astoundingly doubtful about such a

conclusion. Afraid to believe it. And something more: *reluctant* to believe it. Almost . . . disappointed.

And I didn't understand why I wasn't happy instead.

I had never wanted to be from Penikese.

I had never wanted to be born to lepers.

And now I knew that I hadn't been.

If I wanted to, I could climb to the top of Lookout Hill or into the pulpit at Sunday service or up onto the roof of the highest house and yell the news to anyone who would listen.

But I had come to think of my mother as a brave, sad, sick woman. Like Susanna. A woman I wish I'd known.

And for weeks now, whenever I had thought of that woman, I hadn't seen her face. I had seen mine.

I would have to stop that now.

"Please don't tell anyone on Cuttyhunk about this," I said.

At which Miss Maggie raised her eyebrows. "Why not?"

"I'm not sure," I said slowly.

I remembered how it had felt to stand outside the Penikese hospital and learn that some of the lepers had been from islands like Cape Verde and Tobago. That some of them had looked, as I did, like the color Osh made by mixing his rainbow of paints. That real people had lived here. Real people with names like Elvan and Susanna. Not mysteries. Not maybes. Real people. People like me.

But if I was one of those people, could I be an Elizabeth Islander, too?

Or did I have to choose?

"I know what the doctor wrote," I said, looking up at her, "but don't you think it's still possible that I came from Penikese?"

Miss Maggie gave me a rueful smile. "I don't see how," she said. "Is it possible that you would prefer to be from there than from nowhere?"

Maybe. I had to confess: Maybe that was the truth of it. At least part of the truth.

"And why not tell people, regardless?" she asked.

I knew Miss Maggie wouldn't like my answer. She thought that pride was a sin.

"If I wasn't good enough for them before, I don't think I want to be one of them now."

"Oh, but that's a hard thing to say, Crow. And you're not a hard person." She took me by the hand. "If you have a chance to be closer to people, you should take it. And it's not that you weren't good enough," she said. "People are afraid of things they don't understand."

"But why am I hard to understand?" I asked. "They're the ones who are hard to understand. Not me."

"You're not wrong," Miss Maggie said. "But I can't explain what someone else thinks."

"Neither can I," I said. "And I'd rather not twist my brain around trying."

Chapter 13

I carried the letter in my teeth until I was back in the house so I could pass the heavy mussel pail back and forth between my hands.

"Should I start calling you Dog?" Osh asked when I came through the door.

I went straight to him with the letter, which he took from my teeth and held until I had cleaned my hands on a rag and took it back.

"It's from the doctor," I said, putting it on the table.

Osh poured the mussels and their brine into a pot.

I went outside, pulled off my wet clothes, and pegged them on the line. The ones that had sun dried were stiff with salt, but I whipped them against the rocks, salt rising from them in clouds, and put them on.

Osh had left the letter on the table, unopened.

I knew that he wouldn't have read it, even if he could, without asking first.

"Do you want to know what it says?"

He was scrubbing the beards off the mussels and didn't look up from his work. "I suppose I do more than I don't," he said.

I read him the letter, working out the harder words easily because I'd already heard them from Miss Maggie, and then waited for him to say something.

"So you are not from Penikese."

I put the letter back in its envelope. "That's what Miss Maggie said, too, but I don't know. I think maybe I am."

Osh stopped what he was doing, wiped his hands dry, and came to sit with me at the table.

He looked at me intently.

"Why do you say that?"

I shrugged. "Miss Maggie thinks I just want to be from somewhere, anywhere, even a leper colony. But it's not that." I rubbed my forehead with the heel of my hand. "I guess maybe I've thought about the possibility for so long that it feels true now. Except it's more than that." And more than I could put into words.

After a while, he sighed and wove his hands into a basket and said, "You have to be more patient, Crow. What you're doing is confusing. Trying to figure out what's most important to you. What matters. What doesn't. It's all very confusing, I know. Like standing in a hurricane. You have to find a way to step back a little, so you're looking at the storm and not caught up inside it. Otherwise, you might run headlong into something worse."

I thought about that. "Are you telling me to stop looking for my family?"

He closed his eyes. After a moment, he said, "No, Crow. But I do think you should look in as much as you're looking out."

I didn't know what he meant. "I don't know what you mean," I said.

Osh stopped to choose his words. "Sometimes," he said slowly, "people know things. They don't learn them. They don't figure them out. They don't discover them. They *know* them. And it doesn't matter what anyone else has to say about it."

He looked away. "I ended up here because my country was not really my country. It was just where I lived. Where some of us were less than others. Where it was sport, to hurt us."

I waited as quietly as I could. Osh never talked about his life before the island.

"And in the face of that . . . mindless, heartless, stupid rage, I could not protect the people I loved. I begged them to come with me, but they wouldn't. So when I left everything I hated, I also left everything I loved, Crow. Which split me into pieces, like wood for the fire. And I did go into a fire for a while." He sighed. "I had no English when I came to this country. I had no place to live. So I worked in factories, making machines. For so long that I felt like a machine myself. It was either that or starve.

But eventually, I chose starve. I chose a boat with a blue sail. So small. And clean. And quiet. I remember knowing—in that way I'm talking about—that it would take me to another life."

He smiled at me. "And it did. And not much later, you came here, the same way."

"But not because of what *I* knew," I said. "I was just a baby."

"No, that's true. Something else brought you here, but you *know* it. Whatever you might call it." He looked me in the eye. "You can learn things from other people, and you can learn things by keeping your eyes open. But you can learn things from your own self, too. From what your gut tells you. If you pay attention to it," he said.

"But I thought you wanted me to stop being so curious."

Osh sighed deeply. "I did," he said. "But what *I* want is the smallest part of this. I just don't like to think about you out there in the world by yourself."

"Then don't," I said, reaching across the table to put my little hand on his big ones. "I'm not going anywhere."

Dear Miss Evelyn, I wrote later that night on a piece of the special paper Osh used for his paintings. It was thick and beautiful, and I was careful to write slowly and as clearly as I could.

> *Dr. Eastman told me that I could write to you with more questions about Penikese and the babies who were born there: Jason and Morgan.*

I stopped to lick the dry point of my pencil.

I was tempted to write my story, how I had washed ashore in an old skiff, a ruined letter and a ruby ring tucked into my swaddling.

But if Miss Evelyn had any answers for me, she already knew my story. If she didn't, I saw no point in telling her my own private history.

Without telling my story in plain language, I didn't know how to ask the next bit, so I just followed the pencil where it led.

My questions are just words, I wrote. *I wonder if they mean anything to you.*

I stopped again and read back what I'd written. If the paper had not been so dear, I would have ripped it up and started again. Instead, I wrote a list of the words that might open any number of old doors:

Baby, I wrote.
Skiff
Ring
Little feather
Lambs

I thought about the letter in the cinnamon box.

Bright sea, I wrote.

And came up short.

Eight words. Just eight. Almost not worth sending.

I'm sorry if I sound foolish, I wrote. *It's possible that I really am foolish. Thank you.*

And then, taking my cue from Dr. Eastman, I signed the letter:

I remain, Crow.

I didn't understand how I could remain anything *except* Crow, but the letter was done, so I folded it up and set it aside for the morning. Miss Maggie would know how to post it.

"This will cost you," she said, holding up an envelope. "This and the postage."

I nodded. "Chicken coop?"

"Muck it out and load in fresh straw," she said. "Put the muck in a barrow and cart it out behind the barn. And then come on in for lunch when you're done."

I would have done the chore for nothing. For payment for my lessons. For payment for my lunch. But Miss Maggie would never take any pay for those things.

Osh insisted on thanking her with paintings, which she hung all around her house. Above her mantelpiece was a meadow full of sheep. Between her kitchen windows, a skiff riding the current through the Narrows.

The chickens liked me, as long as I didn't bring Mouse along. She didn't mean any harm, but the hens were a ferocious bunch and they always greeted her arrival with a lot of running to and fro, squawking loud enough to wake the dead, and feathers flying.

"Stay out here," I told her. She obliged me by flopping down in the sun and licking the back of one paw, which was her way of saying, "Fine. Chickens smell, anyway."

It *was* pretty smelly in there, and dusty, so I pulled my shirt up over my nose while I worked.

By the time I was done, I was sweaty and stuck all over with straw and feathers.

I spent a moment at Miss Maggie's cistern, dusting myself off and sluicing rainwater over my head, before I met her at her door. She handed me a rag. "You seem to be dripping wet most of the time now," she said. "Dry off before you come inside."

Which I did, and quickly, too, at the smell of chowder on the stove.

She set out two bowls for us, a teacup for Mouse by the door, and biscuits fresh from the oven. They were crisp on the outside, soft and steaming on the inside.

Nothing better than to dredge a hunk of hot biscuit through chowder thick with clams and potatoes.

We ate in silence until Miss Maggie tipped her head toward the letter lying on her sideboard.

"For that nurse?"

I nodded. "I hope you don't mind that I wrote it on my own."

Miss Maggie snorted like Cinders did when she got a gnat up her nose. "What teacher would mind when a student doesn't need her anymore?"

"Oh, that's not it at all," I said. "I need to learn lots of things."

"But how to write a letter is no longer one of them." She added some pepper to her chowder and offered me the mill.

"Do you want to read it?" I asked.

"Is that an invitation?"

I nodded. "There are things I haven't told you yet," I said. "But I'd rather wait until after you've read it."

I watched her open the letter. She raised one eyebrow as she read. Then both.

"This may be the shortest letter I've ever read," she said. "And the most cryptic."

"What's that mean?"

"Mysterious," she replied. "Puzzling."

I imagined that Miss Evelyn in Louisiana might have the same reaction, so I said, "What do you make of it, then?"

Miss Maggie pursed her lips and read the letter through a second time.

"Well," she finally said. "I know why *baby* is on the list. And *skiff*, too. But why the rest? Like *ring*? And *bright sea*?"

So I told her about the ring and the ruined letter that had

come with me in the skiff. "I would have told you sooner, but I only just learned about them myself, before we went to Penikese."

Miss Maggie nodded. "I'm glad you trust me with your secrets," she said. "And I'll keep them."

She ladled some more chowder into my bowl and topped it with a second biscuit. "Now eat up," she said. "There's not nearly enough meat on those bones of yours."

Mouse had finished all of her chowder except for a cube of potato and a coin of carrot, which Miss Maggie saved for the pigs. "As if a morsel of vegetable would kill you," she muttered.

When Miss Maggie turned her back, I slipped Mouse a bit of pork belly from my bowl. She gobbled it down and chased a damselfly out the open door into the yard.

"You'll post this yourself, Crow," Miss Maggie said, tucking my letter into an envelope.

Something I'd never done before. But I seemed to be doing a lot of things for the first time lately. And they'd come out all right, so far.

The post office wasn't much bigger than Miss Maggie's chicken coop but smelled far better, despite Mr. Johnson's cigar.

When he saw Miss Maggie come through the door ahead of me, he said, "Well, good afternoon, Maggie. What can I—" but stopped and said nothing more when I came in behind her and stepped up to the counter.

"I'd like to post another letter," I said, holding it out to him. He didn't take it.

"Maggie," he said, "they sanitized the Penikese mail before they sent it off island. With formaldehyde. And I haven't got any of that."

"This is not Penikese," she said. "Crow has lived here for years now. Are you really going to act this way? With God watching?"

"Now that's not fair, Maggie," he said, "when I've never been anything but decent to you."

"As if that has anything to do with it," she said. "It's Crow who wants to post the letter, not me."

I looked into Mr. Johnson's old blue eyes and said, "I would like to send this to Carville, Louisiana, please."

I set it on the counter.

After a moment, he said, "By airmail again, as before?"

I glanced at Miss Maggie, who nodded briskly.

"Else we'll grow old waiting for a reply," she said.

She paid him for the postage.

And we both watched as he managed to stick on the stamps without touching the envelope.

As we left, I turned back in time to see him shovel my letter into a mail sack, his hand wrapped in newsprint.

And I almost laughed. But I didn't.

Chapter 14

I wonder, sometimes, what would have happened if I hadn't found that little spyglass in the sand. The one I had used for years, searching for whatever I could find.

Since we'd been to Penikese, I hadn't looked to the sea for clues about my past, but on most evenings I still spent an hour atop one hill or another, watching the day go down. And I still carried the spyglass in my pocket, mostly out of habit, partly to be ready in case the wider world decided to show me something new.

It had been just a day since I'd sent the letter to Miss Evelyn, and I was not expecting any reply for a while. Nor was I as anxious as I had been while waiting for the doctor's answer.

I was learning that some things take time, and worrying wouldn't change that.

The day had been soft and fair, and the evening was pink and gold to the west, a dusky blue over the sea.

I wasn't eager for anything more than that.

But when I climbed Lookout Hill, I saw a flash of something white out by Penikese. It had caught what was left of the sun, just for a moment, and then faded.

Through my spyglass, I saw a small sailboat rounding the near point on Penikese, coming from the harbor, a single person at the tiller. As I watched, it headed out into Buzzards Bay, toward the mainland.

I thought it must be the bird keeper. But why would he be heading out into darkness?

When I got home again, wet to my waist, I stripped off all my clothes, pegged them on the line, and spent a moment at one of the rainwater sinks in the near rocks, splashing myself clean for bed.

I dried myself with a towel off the line, so stiff it could have stood up in a breeze. Then I unpegged a fresh nightshirt and shook the stiff out of it and slipped it on.

The glow from the windows was my best welcome.

Osh, mixing paints inside, glanced up and said, "About time you came home."

I sat at the table and patted my knee until Mouse jumped up and told me about her day, turning and turning until she'd settled into my lap.

We watched Osh grinding petals into pulp.

"I saw someone sailing away from Penikese," I said, knuckling Mouse behind her ears.

Osh added a bit of water to the mortar and worked the mash some more.

"The birdman?"

I shrugged. "Who else?"

"*We* went there. Perhaps he had other visitors."

"Maybe."

"Though it's odd they'd be going out in the dark."

"Yes."

Nothing for a while but the muted *tock* of the pestle in the mortar and Mouse's purring.

"I don't think the bird keeper was alone when we went over there," I said. "I heard something in the leper hospital, just before he came around the corner." Again, that small, elusive moment rose through everything that had happened since then, like a bubble in a pot on its way to the boil.

"What did you hear?"

I closed my eyes. "A thump. Like something fell over."

Osh scooped the pulp into a small jar. Orange.

"Maybe he has a cat and it jumped off a bed when we knocked," he said.

I didn't think so. It would have been a very big cat to make such a thump.

I gathered Mouse in my arms, stood up, and dropped her.

She landed with a thump not nearly loud enough.

"*Mouse,*" she said.

But she leaped right back up into my lap the moment I sat down again.

"If it was a cat, it was a tiger," I said.

"Buildings make their own noises sometimes."

I knew that was true, but..."I'd like to go back out there," I said.

Osh glanced my way. "Of course you would."

"We could make it a proper foraging trip," I said. "Come back with a whole bag of woadwaxen."

"Tomorrow we pull traps," he said. The mainlanders were coming over in numbers now and would be looking for lobster tails to bait their hooks.

"For how long?"

"The morning. I expect rain in the afternoon." Osh was known for such predictions, most of which came true. "And I don't see the point of sailing back there because of a thump you think you heard."

"A thump I *did* hear," I said. "And a chance to go into the cottages, maybe."

He shook his head. "I don't see the point of that, either. What do you expect to find?"

I watched him wipe out the mortar and fill it with the woadwaxen I'd collected on Penikese. "I don't know," I said.

Which, oddly, drew a nod. "We'll sail to the harbor when we have time," Osh said. "But if the birdman's boat is there, we'll sail straight back."

"But—"

"Straight back," he said. "No sense in pestering a man with a gun."

In the morning, we sailed out to pull our lobster pots. Osh turned into the wind at each float so the skiff went into irons, its sails limp and luffing, and then tethered us to the buoy and hauled the pot up, hand over hand, and into the boat so I could reach in and grab the lobster while it clacked its claws and arched its back, flapping its tail madly.

I'd been pinched in the process, more often than I liked, so I'd learned some tricks over the years. It had been a while since a lobster had last caught me in its claws.

After I emptied each pot, Osh baited it with a fish head and tossed it out again.

And we sailed to the next float, checked it for the mark that meant it was one of ours, and repeated the process.

In the early days, I had worried that someone else would take our lobsters, but Osh said that the Elizabeths were like the Wild West, where stealing a horse meant hanging.

"No one poaches," he said. "Not here. If a float has my mark, the trap below has my lobster. And no funny business."

I liked the idea that no one would steal another person's livelihood, even though they could do it in the dark of night, unseen. Even though lobsters could not tell tales.

It was a code we lived by, and I respected that, but I confess that I found it odd how the same people who followed these unwritten rules sometimes ignored the ones spelled out in their sacred pages.

Chapter 15

*B*y the time we sailed through the Narrows and into the harbor, we had twelve big lobsters in a bushel basket fitted with a lid.

Osh pulled up the centerboard as we came into shore alongside the fish pier.

I lowered the sail and scrambled out of the skiff, towing it into the shallows, where Osh stepped out and hoisted the dripping basket onto his shoulder.

I pulled the skiff higher onto the sand and tied it to a post. Then I followed Osh up the pier lane toward the grocery.

I expected to find some islanders on the porch, sharing news and gossip, and maybe even a few summer people come to start the season early. I often saw them at the grocery, packing picnic baskets with bottles of cold soda pop and thick sandwiches. The ladies in pretty dresses and straw hats. The men in dark trousers, white jackets, and fedoras.

But there were no summer people on the porch when we arrived. Just Mr. Benson, who was one of the many Cuttyhunk pilots who guided ships coming through the Graveyard.

As Osh climbed the steps to the porch, Mr. Benson said, "Daniel."

Osh said, "Benson."

I stayed in the yard, on the other side of the porch rail, out of habit. "Morning, Crow," Mr. Benson said. He was sitting in one of the rockers, packing his pipe with tobacco from a pouch.

"Good morning, Mr. Benson."

Osh left the lobsters on the porch and went inside to settle up with Mr. Higgins, the grocer. He usually took his pay in trade: flour, coffee, spice, dried beans, and canned goods; or put it on account for a day when we needed more than lobsters would buy.

"I hear you been to Penikese," Mr. Benson said. He looked at me curiously. "And writing letters to the doctor that used to be there."

I wasn't sure I liked people knowing my business. I hated the thought of the islanders talking about me as if I were news.

Before I could decide how to reply, Mr. Benson went on to say, "The gamekeeper over there said the doctor disinfected every last thing before he left. Don't know why he'd bother. They shoulda burned every bit of it down straightaway."

He seemed to be saying that nothing from that place should be allowed to remain, though I'd never known him to be mean.

"The bird keeper told you that? About the leper doctor?" I said.

Mr. Benson nodded. "He moved into the hospital after they cleaned it up. Used to come over from time to time for a square meal and a chat, though he hasn't been lately." He gave a snort of laughter. "Perfect fellow for the job. Looks like a sandpiper, head to toe."

"How do you mean?"

"Little, skinny fella," Mr. Benson said. "With a nose like a beak."

I pictured the big, flat-faced man we'd met on Penikese.

"From down south?" I said.

Mr. Benson shook his head. "A Mainer," he said, "born and bred."

Not the birdman we'd met out there. Not even close.

Osh came through the door with a sack of groceries. "Benson," he said, passing by.

"Daniel," Mr. Benson said, nodding. "Crow."

And we headed back down the lane toward the skiff.

I let my feet decide where to put themselves as I followed Osh down to the beach, my mind busy with other things.

If the bird keeper was a little fellow from Maine, then who was the big southern man we'd met?

As we sailed back through the Narrows and toward home, I told Osh what Mr. Benson had said.

"Maybe the old bird keeper left and the one we met came out to take his place," Osh said.

Which was possible, I supposed.

But my gut told me a different story, and I decided to listen to it.

———

It did rain that afternoon and all night into morning, too. Not a gale. Just a long, gray rain that fell straight and soft on a flat sea.

Osh decided I should go to Miss Maggie's for lessons. "She'll come out here if you don't go there first," he said, and I knew he was right. Rain always brought her to our door, draped in a long oilskin, skirts wet from crossing over. "Save her from getting soaked."

So I put on my own poncho, pulled up the hood, and headed out into the gray. It was mid-tide, so I was not much wet when I made land and was otherwise dry inside my poncho. The rain on my hood made the world very small, and I found myself filled with thoughts as I walked.

When I reached Miss Maggie's place, it was empty, which was odd on a day like this. "Miss Maggie!" I called, wandering around to the barn and in where the horses and the cows stayed dry on days like this. Mouse was waiting for me in one of the stalls, curled up in the manger. "*Mouse*," she said when she saw me lean in over the half door.

"Good morning, Mouse," I said. "Good morning, Cinders,"

which she answered with a snort and a shake of her head. "Where's Miss Maggie?"

But they either did not know or would not answer.

I asked her milk cows, too, but they just blinked their big, peaceful eyes at me.

I looked all around the barn, calling, but no one else was there.

At the big door I could see sheep grazing in the distance and, beyond them, Miss Maggie, coming home.

I went out to meet her halfway.

With all the rain and the hood shadowing her face, I couldn't see her tears, but I could hear her crying. Her hands were brown with mud.

"Hawks," she said. "Or maybe an owl. Something got Snowdrop. And she's dead." She was talking about the littlest of the lambs, still small and frail while the others had grown to be sturdy young sheep, full of play. Miss Maggie rarely named the lambs, since it was harder to butcher something with a name. But she'd intended to keep Snowdrop for her wool alone. Now, something else had done the butchering.

"I buried what was left of her," Miss Maggie said, marching past me. "Come help me with the grooming."

As I followed her toward the barn, I thought of the headstone on Penikese. The little lamb carved there. And suddenly my own twelve years felt like a long time, as if I were young and old at once.

Inside the barn, we shed our ponchos and, armed with a curry comb and a dandy brush, each took a horse, Cinders for me, a roan named Clover, in the next stall, for Miss Maggie.

We talked while we worked, mostly because we had things to say but also because it calmed the horses. They loved the grooming, but sometimes they were a little shy of the dandy brush when we came close to tender spots.

I told Miss Maggie about the sailboat leaving Penikese at dusk and how Mr. Benson had described the gamekeeper. "That man we met was no sandpiper," I said. "More like a bulldog."

"Well, it's odd, I'll admit that, but does it matter?" she said. "I don't see what any of that has to do with you or what you went there for."

So I told her about the thump I'd heard at the hospital.

"Osh thought it might be a cat jumping or the building making its own noise," I said, "but I don't think so."

Silence for a while. Nothing but the sound of the horses shifting as we worked, Miss Maggie sneezing at the dust stirred up by the dandy brush.

Then, "So what do you intend to do about it?" she said.

I didn't need to think about my answer. "Go back out there," I said. "And look some more."

"For what?"

"For whatever I can," I said. "There's something I'm supposed to do. I just don't know what it is."

After a bit, Miss Maggie said, "Perhaps it's time to let that go. Maybe tell your heart to listen to your brain for a change."

I didn't much like that advice.

I soaked a rag, wrung it out, and began to wash Cinder's face. "Why were you crying about Snowdrop?" I asked.

After a moment, Miss Maggie stepped into the doorway of the stall. "Of all people, you should know the answer to that."

I stopped what I was doing and turned to face her.

"I do," I said.

She looked at me for a long moment.

"All right," she finally said, nodding.

She returned to Clover, and I could hear him shifting and sighing as she worked on his dusty coat.

"When do you mean to go back out there?" she said through the wall.

"As soon as the rain stops."

After a moment, she appeared in the doorway again. "I'll be waiting at the Neck," she said briskly. "And tell Osh the garden can look after itself for a little while."

"The garden needs tending," Osh said when I proposed sailing to Penikese as soon as the weather cleared.

"Miss Maggie said it can look after itself for a while."

He was filling a pail with wood ash from the fireplace. He used it to feed the plants and frustrate the slugs.

"She did, did she?" He climbed to his feet and dusted off his hands. "And I suppose she'll be coming with us again?"

There. He *would* go. I smiled. "Of course," I said. "Like the Musketeers."

"All for one," he said.

"She'll be waiting at the Neck when it stops raining," I said.

And, later that day, when the clouds tore apart in the freshening breeze, she was.

Chapter 16

I was relieved when we sailed into Penikese Harbor and saw no boat at the pier. We hadn't seen one sailing nearby, either, so I expected we'd have the place to ourselves. For a while at least.

"The birdman hasn't come back, then," I said.

Osh said, "Not yet."

He climbed out of the skiff and offered a hand to Miss Maggie, who surprised me by taking it. I followed, and we pulled the boat up on the sand.

"So, here we are," Osh said. "What now?"

"We find out what made that thump."

"I didn't come for the thump," he said. "I came for woad-waxen." He'd brought a canvas sack this time.

"I'll help with that," Miss Maggie said. "You go on ahead, Crow. We'll see you there."

"But any sign of that man and back you come," Osh said.

I promised I would. And I meant it. That birdman was a scary fellow, and I had no intention of meeting up with him again.

I started off walking but was soon running down the old grassy lane, up and over the hills at speed, fueled by a strong mix of curiosity, a little fear, and what my legs wanted.

In no time at all, I was at the hospital, Miss Maggie and Osh still foraging in the distance.

I climbed the steps to the porch and knocked on the big door. Softly at first, then harder.

Again, from somewhere inside, a noise. This time a series of smaller thumps, like someone was knocking in return.

This time, the door was not locked.

I pushed it open. "Hello!" I called. "Hello?"

From above I heard the knocking sound again. And something else: a muffled growling.

I pictured a huge dog, hungry for someone like me to open a door and set it free.

I thought about waiting for Osh and Miss Maggie.

I turned to go back into the yard until they arrived.

But then I heard a bigger thump and something breaking, and I hurried into the hospital and up the front stairs without another thought.

"Hello?" I called as I climbed.

The knocking sound drew me toward a long hallway, all its doors closed.

I opened the first one to find nothing but an old bed frame and a small table topped with a washbowl and pitcher.

I stood in the hallway, listening, and then crept past the next two doors to where the knocking was loudest.

I admit that I was scared as I reached for the knob.

And I was scared as I slowly pushed the door open.

And I was scared when I saw who was waiting for me inside, though more for him than for myself.

There, on the floor, was a man rolled up in a bedsheet, from his chin to his ankles, and tied tight in a rope, too. His mouth was stuffed full of rag tied in place with a kerchief so all he could do was growl and moan. Only his feet were free to move at all. It was his boot, its hard edge tapping on the floor, that I had heard from below.

Beside him were an overturned table and a broken pitcher.

When he saw me in the doorway, he closed his eyes and went limp and quiet but for a pitiful sobbing deep in his throat.

I removed the gag first, as quickly as I could, and threw it aside.

The man began to cry properly when I did, gasping and sobbing so hard that I couldn't understand a word he was saying.

I realized that I was talking, too, as I tried to free him. "It's all right now," I said, over and over again. "It's all right now, mister. It's all right now."

"I don't know you. I don't know you," he stammered as I worked on the knots in the rope. "Is he—where is he? Is he gone?"

"He's not here," I said. "I'm Crow. And I'm going to get you out of here."

The sheet was filthy, soaked with all the things a body does, and the stench in the room was terrible. I pulled apart the knots in the rope that bound him and rolled him gently until he was free of the sheet and could finally move, which he did slowly and carefully after being bound for days.

I stood back and watched him work the blood into his arms and legs, flex his fingers, crane his neck this way and that, crying all the while.

He was a small man. Thin. With a sharp nose. Like a bird.

"You're the bird keeper," I said.

He quieted down at that, rubbing his face with his hands and sighing again and again.

"I am," he said, his voice hoarse. "Would you please step out for a moment. Please. I wonder, would you step out, please." And he began to cry again, but less urgently.

I went back into the hallway and closed the door behind me.

After a bit, he opened it again and stood there, wrapped in a blanket, his clothes on the floor in a heap behind him.

"Are you—" I began, but he held up one hand and edged past me, down the hallway and then the stairs as I followed, out through the door and across the yard, faster and faster, and over the edge of the bluff as I watched, across the rocky beach, falling twice but scrambling again to his feet, shedding the blanket as he went, and straight into the sea.

I followed him, gathering up the blanket and shaking it

clean, while he splashed madly in the waves and then sat in the shallows and scrubbed himself with wet sand, head to toe.

Then he slowly rolled onto his knees and worked his way carefully to his feet, covering his private parts with his hands.

He was terribly thin and pale.

Blood from his falls trickled down his wet legs, one knee already swelling.

I handed him the blanket and turned my back.

"Grab hold of my shoulder," I said. "I'll go slowly."

His hand felt like a claw.

Several times, as we made our way over the rocks, he nearly fell, and I knew I'd have bruises on my shoulder from his grip.

I heard Osh calling my name and I called back, "Here! Here!" as loudly as I could, but when the gamekeeper gasped and began to tremble, I said, "It's all right. That's Osh. That's just Osh," but he refused to take another step until Osh and Miss Maggie appeared at the top of the bluff.

When they saw us among the rocks below, they hurried down, Osh taking the gamekeeper in his arms and carrying him like a child onto the soft sand at the foot of the bluff, where he laid him down.

Miss Maggie dropped to her knees beside him and tucked the blanket around the man, who was shivering, though the day was warm. "My Lord, you're nothing but skin and bones," she said, pulling off her hat and tucking it beneath his head. "What happened to you?"

Osh stood tall above us, watching, listening.

I kept one eye on the bay, the other on the man's face as he slowly began to collect himself and eventually said, "I'm Sloan. The gamekeeper."

"*You're* the gamekeeper? Not that other man?" Osh said.

Mr. Sloan shook his head. "Last time I sailed to New Bedford for supplies a man at the wharf asked for a lift to Cuttyhunk. Said he was a pilot coming over for work. And I thought nothing of it. Didn't mind the extra mile to drop him there before coming home. Thought I'd stop at the inn for a meal and some company."

He stopped and sat up, the sand making his wet hair white. Pulled the blanket tighter around his shoulders and drew a long, shaky breath.

"But when we were halfway across the bay he told me he wanted to go to Penikese instead. Said he had some business here, which made me laugh. 'What business?' I asked him. 'There's no business on Penikese but birds and rabbits.' To which he said I could either take him here or he'd throw me into the bay and leave me to drown."

Mr. Sloan shook his head sadly. "I'm not a big person. Or young anymore. And I can't swim a lick. So I brought him to Penikese, God forgive me. I'm not sure I would have, though, if I'd known how long he'd keep me locked up while he did . . . I don't know what. I don't understand what he was doing here. Or why he had to pen me up like that. For what?"

"We don't know," Miss Maggie said.

"Or why he tied and gagged me every time he went out any-where," he continued, as if she hadn't said anything. "I ask you," and here he looked at each of us in turn, "where was I going to run to? And who was going to hear me call?"

"We would have," I said. "When we were here the first time."

"That was you?" he asked. "Then, too?"

Miss Maggie nodded. "We sailed over from Cuttyhunk. We . . . had business of our own."

Mr. Sloan sighed. "I heard you knocking. I was tied to a chair and I tipped it over, to make some noise. Hoping you would hear me."

Miss Maggie looked at Osh and he at her.

"She heard you," Miss Maggie said, nodding at me, "but that man came just then and ran us off. I'm sorry we didn't come back sooner."

But Mr. Sloan shook his head. "No, it's better that you didn't. He was different after that. Worse. And angry. No telling what he would have done if you'd come back."

He worked his way back up to his feet. "If you don't mind, could we maybe go somewhere else now?" He looked around fearfully and began to stagger up the bluff. "I have some clean clothes in the hospital, but there's nothing else I need so much as to be off this island before he comes back."

Osh helped him to the hospital, and we waited outside while he went in alone.

It took him no time at all to dress himself and pack his bag and join us again in the yard. He looked better in clean clothes, though some blood was seeping through at the knee and his hair was still wild with sand and salt.

"I owe you a debt," he said. "I would have died here if you hadn't come."

Miss Maggie ran a hand over my head. "You can thank this one," she said. "She's the reason we came back."

"And I will," said Mr. Sloan. "You just tell me how and I will."

"On Cuttyhunk," Osh said, turning toward the harbor. "Time to go."

But I had one more thing to do first. "I'll catch up with you," I said. "I just want to look in the cottages. For a minute. That's all."

Osh nodded. Miss Maggie said, "For a minute. But no more. And then you come along."

"What's there that you want?" Mr. Sloan said. "Those old shacks are empty and not a thing left in them."

But he turned without waiting for an answer and followed Osh and Miss Maggie slowly down the lane.

The first cottage was just as Mr. Sloan had said. Empty. No furniture. No curtains in the windows. Even the stove was gone, nothing left but a hole in the ceiling where the pipe had been.

Worse, someone had pulled up the floorboards so nothing remained except the frame.

I imagined that they'd gone to feed the big fires that had burned outside the hospital. For roasting geese, I had supposed.

Beneath where the floor had been, the dirt was all dug up.

More holes.

I closed the door behind me and headed for next cottage.

Like the first, this one had no furniture or floor at all. And, as before, the ground was all holes and mounds of loose dirt.

I wondered what he had been digging for.

And whether he had found it.

This time, I carefully stepped between the holes and made my way around the cottage, looking for whatever wanted to be found.

If I hadn't, I wouldn't have seen what was carved on the wall in one corner, just level with my eyes.

Another lamb.

Beside it, someone had carved something else.

A feather.

I remembered the ruined letter that had been stuck to my tiny chest. Its "lambs." Its "little feather."

I heard Osh calling me in the distance.

I ran my fingers over the lamb. It was no bigger than my open hand. And the feather, no bigger than my finger.

"Coming!" I yelled back.

I left the cottage and took off at a run, down the lane and straight to where the others waited for me, all of us eager to be going now.

I did not know what I was leaving behind, still undiscovered.

Or what else was waiting, across the water, on the mainland.

Chapter 17

On the crossing from Penikese, Mr. Sloan huddled in the stern, shivering and ducking at the mere suggestion of spray coming over the bow, and I felt guilty at the pleasure of a warm June afternoon while he suffered.

"Miss Maggie makes the best soup in the world," I said. "She'll fix you up in no time."

When I said the word *soup*, Mr. Sloan finally smiled. "I would be obliged," he said, "for even an old ear of corn. Soup would be heaven."

Miss Maggie gave him a wry look. "Far from that," she said, "but it should help put you right."

"Here," Osh said, pulling a twist of oil cloth from his pocket. Inside was a stash of jerky he carried, just in case.

Mr. Sloan unwrapped it and immediately tore off a bite, chewing hard, and closed his eyes, holding the jerky in both hands near his mouth, like a squirrel with the last of the winter nuts.

When we reached Cuttyhunk, I ran ahead to fetch Cinders so Mr. Sloan wouldn't have to walk, while Miss Maggie went to the post office where Mr. Johnson kept the telegraph machine. We all knew that he'd send for the police in Falmouth and then, with his next breath, begin to spread the news that Mr. Sloan had been held captive in the leprosarium by a mysterious southerner.

The islanders were used to calamity. When a hurricane blew through, as one had just a year before—tearing off roofs and casting boats up on the shore—everyone suffered at least a little. And when a ship wrecked in the Graveyard, people sometimes died—mariners or lifesavers or both—and everyone on the Elizabeths felt the stab of such disaster.

This was different.

When word got out about Mr. Sloan, excitement would spread like heat lightning across the islands.

There would be talk of nothing else.

"What was he digging for?" I asked Mr. Sloan as we all sat at Miss Maggie's table, eating soup and bread. There wasn't much in the garden yet beyond spring onions and baby kale, but she still had some potatoes and carrots in the root cellar, and cooking had brought them back to life. So had butter. And I believe that Mr. Sloan would have eaten an old shoe if she'd served it to him hot.

He sounded a little like Mouse while he ate, purring and blinking as he bent low over the steam rising from his bowl.

"Let the poor man eat," Miss Maggie said. "You can ask him questions later."

But Mr. Sloan shook his head. "No, please, it's quite all right. I'm happy to tell you what I know."

He sat up straight. "What was he digging for?" he repeated thoughtfully. "I didn't know that he *was* digging. I saw him only when he came to leave food every morning and take away my . . . chamber pot." He turned pink and looked away from Miss Maggie. "I'm sorry, ma'am."

"Nothing to be sorry about," she said with a frown.

"He dug holes all over the island and even in the cottages," I said.

Which seemed to surprise Mr. Sloan, but then he nodded and said, "Which must be why he stayed on Penikese for so long. He was digging up the island. But what for?"

"Treasure, maybe?" I said.

Which drew something like a laugh from Mr. Sloan. "What treasure? Lots of geese on Penikese but none of them laying golden eggs."

"So you can't say if he found anything before he left?"

Mr. Sloan shook his head. "All I can tell you is that he was cruel. And more than cruel, for leaving me to die when he might have set me free before he sailed off in my boat. I couldn't have chased him. And he busted up my radio so I couldn't call for help. No one would have come to Penikese for days, maybe weeks. He could have gotten clean away." He swallowed hard and I was afraid he might start to cry again.

"That's enough now," Miss Maggie said.

But Mr. Sloan held up his hand and said, "Oh, I'm all right. A little talk won't do me any harm."

He nodded to me and spooned up some more soup.

"You don't know anything more about him?" I asked.

He paused, looking back. "I can tell you what he asked me," he said. "When we first landed on Penikese, he pulled me ashore and to the top of the bluff there by the pier and said, 'Where did she live?'"

"Where did who live?" I asked.

"That's exactly what I said! Those very words. And he replied, 'The leper,' as if there were only one. As if I knew anything at all about those people." He raised his eyebrows and shook his head. "It was long after they left before I went over to live."

"And then what happened?" I asked.

"I told him I didn't know a thing about the lepers except where they'd lived and died. I showed him both places. The hospital and the cottages. The graveyard. And then he looked around and back at me and said, 'What about the nurse?'"

Mr. Sloan shook his head again. "I think he was a bit daft. Or he just didn't understand that I hadn't been there when the others were. I *told* him that. I told him *again* that I didn't know *anything* about a nurse or the lepers or anything else about any other humans who had ever lived on Penikese. Period."

Mr. Sloan ate the last of his soup and bread and leaned back with a sigh. "But that wasn't good enough for him."

At this point, Miss Maggie fetched some bandages and told Mr. Sloan to roll up his pant legs so she could have a look at his scrapes.

Osh and I grinned at each other as he tried to put her off and she bullied him into it. "If you insist," he finally said, baring his knees.

I washed out my bowl and stood in the doorway waiting for Osh, but he tipped his chin at me and said, "Go on home. I'll be staying here."

Miss Maggie looked at him curiously.

"In the barn," he said, turning his hat in his hands.

"I'll be fine," Miss Maggie said.

"Just the same," Osh said.

Mr. Sloan closed his eyes and began, very softly, to snore.

"*Help me get him to bed and I can promise you he'll sleep till morning*," she whispered.

"Just the same," Osh said again. "I'll be nearby if you need anything."

He came to stand with me. "Will you be all right by yourself?"

To be honest, I didn't much like the idea of being alone like that and I nearly said so. But I did like how Osh wanted to look after Miss Maggie. And I did like how he knew I could look after myself.

"I'll be fine," I said. I touched his sleeve. "Will you come home in the morning or will I come to you?"

He put his hand on my head. "I'll be home at first light," he said.

I had never said such a good-bye to Osh, but I said it now and went out through the door without him.

It was odd to spend the night alone on our island. Mouse tried to take Osh's place by saying very little and sitting quietly among his painting things.

I lit a lantern when it got dark and carried it with me wherever I went, which wasn't very far in such a small place. My bed was in one corner, Osh's in another. The rest of the space was for cooking and sitting, a table and an easel.

Our washtub, where we occasionally did a proper laundry, followed by a proper bath, was outside. So was our fishing gear. And everything else.

I sat by the cold fireplace and considered reading a book, but I'd read everything I had. I thought about practicing my sums, but that seemed a poor way to spend this unusual solitude.

What, I wondered, was done best alone? That, I decided, was what I should do.

But there was nothing I could do that was not better with Osh there.

And so I started to think.

Not about anything in particular.

I didn't try to solve a problem. Or chase an idea. Or invent a notion.

I just let my mind drift. And I let my body follow it. First, in the chair by the fireplace. Then at the window, looking at the sea.

Then out through the door and onto the beach, to lie in the cool sand, my head pillowed on my laced hands.

Mouse followed me, though not in a straight line, and then sat next to my head and licked her paws until something scuttled through the grasses nearby, and she gave chase.

The stars were enormous. They pulsed as if they were breathing.

I heard something splash offshore. A bass, perhaps. Or a diving bird.

A huge sand flea, heavy as a pebble, jumped first onto my chest and then onto my cheek, and I lurched upward, batting it away before it could bite me.

I rubbed the spot where it had landed.

Beneath my fingers, my skin was soft and cool. Smooth. Even the little birthmark on my cheek.

The little feather.

The little feather I'd always had.

Even before I'd drifted to this shore.

Chapter 18

I stood up, very still in the darkness. The sea was louder than it had been a moment before. The stars bigger.

I went carefully back inside the cottage, retrieved the lantern, set it carefully on my small table next to my bed.

The cinnamon box was on my windowsill.

I opened it slowly. Took out the letter. Unfolded it. Held it in the lantern light and read again:

if I could
for now
hope you
bright sea
better off
lambs
little feather

I left something
day it might help

I remembered the carvings on the wall of the cottage on Penikese. A small lamb. Alongside it, a little feather.

I put the letter back in the box. Carried the lantern to our one small mirror. Turned my face. Examined the mark on my cheek.

A little feather.

Dr. Eastman had written that there was no third baby. Just one sent to New Bedford. One buried.

But the letter in my hand, as ruined as it was, told me a different story.

I read it again. And again.

Then I took its mysteries to bed with me. And found them waiting in the morning, right where I'd left them.

I was up and washed and dressed and out the door before daylight was more than a pale idea.

I met Osh beyond the bass stands, coming home.

He stopped at the sight of me.

"Miss me, did you?" he said, almost smiling.

I nodded. It was true. I had.

But that was not all.

"I think I know who my real parents are," I said.

And the almost smile was gone, as if it had never been.

He walked past me, past the bass stands, down over the bluff and across the sand bridge that was nearly dry for once, the tide dead low.

"You'd best be along to Miss Maggie's," he said brusquely as I hurried to keep up with him. "The police will be there soon. You and Mr. Sloan can tell your tales together."

Outside the house, he stopped only to grab a bait net and a pail before heading for the tidal pools at the base of the rocks where minnows and sand eels often found themselves stranded.

He began to scoop them up and into the pail. They flashed silver in the early light.

"Osh," I said. "What's the matter?"

But he didn't answer me.

"Are you angry?" Though I couldn't see why he would be.

He looked at me and away again.

"I'm not angry," he said. "Do what you have to do."

"I will," I replied. "Like you said I should. You said I should pay attention to things. Remember?"

"I do," he said.

"Then why are you upset with me?"

He looked at me, full on, and I could see how sad he was.

"Am I not real?" he said.

I didn't understand what he was saying until I realized what I myself had said.

"Osh, you are the most real thing in the world."

"But I'm not your father," he said.

"Of course you are," I said. "But you're not my only father. And you're not my mother."

"I know that," he said.

But he turned back to his work until I said, "The letter you gave me. It said *little feather*. And there was a carving in one of the cottages on Penikese," I said, grabbing at his arm. "Osh, stop."

Which he finally did, with a sigh.

He turned the net inside out, dumping three sand eels into the pail and then sluicing in some water so they could breathe. He set it aside and sat down on a nearby rock. I sat next to him. The rock was cold and a little wet and not at all comfortable.

"I found a carving of a lamb in the cottage, like the one on the grave marker but smaller," I said. "And next to it a carving of a little feather."

Osh looked at me intently. "Like the one on your cheek?" he said.

I nodded.

"You think that means something."

I nodded again, more slowly. "I do," I said.

Osh moved his pail into a bigger wedge of shadow so the fish would stay cool.

"I suppose it might," he said.

"Two lambs. Two feathers, one of them right here." I touched my cheek. "Patients came from all over the world to Penikese. From islands off Africa. Off South America. Where people have skin more like mine than yours. And one of them was a mother who lost one child to the mainland, to an orphanage, where he had nobody at all."

I felt as if I would cry, but I tried hard not to. "If you were that little baby's father, would you be able to send another one off to live all by herself, same as the first?"

Osh shook his head. "I would not," he said. "No matter who was willing to take her."

I took his hand in mine.

"I think this little feather on my cheek means something. I think it means the second baby didn't die. I think it means they sent that baby to sea in an old skiff and didn't tell anybody. I think it means that the grave with the lamb marker is an empty grave."

He looked down and away.

I thought about the graveyard on Penikese.

"If I'm right, then my parents are dead," I said. "The lepers who are buried out there. Susanna and . . ."

"Elvan." He looked sad now in a different way. He laid his open hand on my cheek. "I'm so sorry if that's true," he said.

"It's all right," I said. "You had nothing to do with anything except saving me."

Osh looked at me curiously. "You wanted to prove that you weren't from Penikese," he said, "but now you seem almost glad to think that you are, Crow."

"I know," I said. "I am. But that doesn't make any sense. Why would I want that? To have parents who died from a terrible disease? To have parents who had sent me out to sea in a leaky skiff? When I was just a new baby?"

Osh smiled at me, but it was a sad smile. "They had the best of all possible reasons for doing that," he said. "For trusting the sea to take you safely away and deliver you safely to a different shore."

"What reason?"

"They loved you, Crow. They didn't want you to become ill, like they were. And you said it yourself: They knew how lonely Jason was in that orphanage and they wanted something better for you."

He wasn't smiling anymore when he said, "I wonder what he'll do when he finds out he has a sister."

Chapter 19

I helped Osh catch bait for a while and then ate some porridge with him, a little honey on top, before I went out to tend the garden, so consumed with my thoughts that the chore was done and over with before I knew it.

I poked my head in the door and said, "I'm going to Miss Maggie's before I dig clams. Do you want to come along?"

"I do," he replied, "but not until after the police have left. I'll fish for a while. You go on. But here," he said. "Give them this." He handed me a piece of paper rolled into a tube and tied with a bit of string.

"What is it?" I asked.

"That man," he said. "Don't get it wet."

I held it high as I waded through the incoming tide. Then I followed the lane up toward town, turning off at the path to Miss Maggie's.

There were two policemen in her kitchen, one old and short, the other young and tall. Both were clean shaven. They wore identical uniforms with lots of pockets and buttons and belts. They both carried pistols.

"Who's this?" the tall one asked when I stepped through the open door to find them there.

"This," she said, "is Crow. The reason Mr. Sloan is alive. Crow, these are Officers Kelly"—she gestured at the tall one—"and Reardon."

"Hello," I said.

They nodded to me and turned back to Mr. Sloan, who was sitting at the kitchen table looking younger and happier after a night's sleep.

I stood in the corner and listened as he finished telling them what he'd told us the night before.

And Miss Maggie described the holes all over the island.

And then I told them how even the floors in the cottages had been pulled up.

"Crow here thinks he was looking for treasure," Mr. Sloan said.

Officer Kelly snorted. "I think somebody's been reading too many adventure stories," he said.

But he had not seen the crown that had come up on an anchor fluke. Or the giant silver buckle. Or my little gold ring in the cinnamon box.

Mr. Sloan said, "I agree, it sounds far-fetched, but why else would he be digging up an island? And one in the waters where pirates used to sail?"

Which drew a thoughtful look from Officer Reardon. "Pirate treasure?" he said. "Out on Penikese?"

Mr. Sloan shrugged. "That man kept me prisoner while he spent a lot of time and effort digging up that island. What for, otherwise?"

When the officers asked Mr. Sloan to describe the man who'd so mistreated him, he did, pretty well; but I handed Miss Maggie the scroll from Osh, and she, after unrolling it, handed it to them.

"The spittin' image," Mr. Sloan said when he saw the portrait that Osh had sketched. "Right down to that look in his eye. Mean, he was."

"Did you make this?" Officer Reardon asked me.

I laughed at the idea. "No, that was Osh."

They looked at me sternly. "Osh," I said.

"He's an artist," Miss Maggie said. "He sailed us to Penikese that day and saw the man, too."

Officer Kelly rolled up the sketch.

Officer Reardon closed his little notebook and tucked it in his pocket. "We'll do what we can to find him," he said, "but he's had a good head start and could be anywhere by now."

Mr. Sloan sighed. "Far from here, I hope, though I'd like him caught. Will you take me to the mainland with you?"

They would, they said.

"Thank you, Miss Crow," Mr. Sloan said as he left. "And you, Miss Maggie. And please thank Mr. Osh as well."

And off he went, an officer on either side of him, bound for Woods Hole and other birds in other places.

⁓

"So sad to think you might be theirs," Miss Maggie said when I told her what the little feather on my cheek might mean. We were in her garden, planting more corn and beans that would continue to bear after the crops we'd planted in May were done. "Their first child was sent away into a lonely life. I suppose it makes sense that they decided to send their second child to something better, maybe." She shook her head. "But to sea? Alone? So small?"

I felt fierce about this, that they had done me no harm, and I wanted to give her just one answer to all three questions: *They had no choice.*

"Perhaps they felt they had no other choice," Miss Maggie said, and I loved her for it. "But it breaks my heart to think of them tying you into that old skiff and pushing you out onto the tide. Carving a headstone for an empty grave to convince people that their baby had died."

"If they hadn't, someone might have come looking for me. And sent me to the orphanage in New Bedford, like Jason."

She nodded. "Perhaps." She handed me a tray of bean sprouts and pointed to an empty row. "Start these over there."

While I planted the young beans, I tried to imagine life in

that orphanage. I tried to imagine Jason there, all alone, for years. No one brave enough or kind enough to touch him.

"I want to find my brother," I said.

Miss Maggie looked up from her work. "You think you'll be able to find him after all this time? He's probably"—she thought about it—"nearly twenty years old by now. Long since on his own."

"But maybe still in New Bedford," I said. "The orphanage might know where. Why not try to find him?"

She wiped a wisp of hair off her forehead with the back of her hand. "I don't know," she said slowly. "He may have found his own way. He may be happy with his life the way it is."

I shrugged. "Why wouldn't he be even happier if he knew about me?"

She kept her eyes on what she was doing. "I don't know," she said again. "But if you're set on this, I'll help. If you want."

"And Osh, too," I said.

"Of course." She folded the dirt over a trough of seeds and stood up, dusting off her hands. "There's no going without him."

Chapter 20

"I haven't left the islands since I got here," Osh said, "and I don't plan to now."

He'd caught a striper for our supper and another for Miss Maggie. He had scaled and cleaned them, sliced the cheeks from ours, and was wrapping hers in brown paper.

"But we won't be gone for long," I said. "Just a few hours."

"That's an eight-mile crossing," he said, tying the package up in white string. "Nine, into the harbor. Who knows how far by foot to the orphanage. And then a long trip back. It's a day at least. More if the weather turns."

He stowed the paper and string, shoved some driftwood into the stove, and blew on the lazy coals until they glowed.

"But that's not so long," I said. "A day. Why can't we go, even if it does take a day?"

"I have chores. And you do, too, and your lessons, besides, which you have been neglecting."

Odd, coming from Osh, who left my schooling to me.

He put an iron pan on the stove, added butter and spring onions, and, after a bit, tossed in the bass cheeks. The smell, the sizzle, brought Mouse running.

Osh gave her a bit of raw belly meat instead. She rolled onto her back and gripped the meat in both paws as she ate it.

"If you had a brother somewhere and might be able to find him, wouldn't you go looking?" I asked.

Osh went still. Only the knife in his hand trembled a little.

When he moved, it was to tend the cheeks in the pan before they burned.

"I'm sorry," I said. "I wasn't thinking."

I fetched a plate for us to share. Forks. Salt and pepper. Cistern water in a single mug. The last of a loaf of molasses bread.

He slid the cheeks onto the plate and poured the butter and onions on top.

We sat down. Ate. It was wonderful. I told Osh so.

"Things are usually better when you don't mess with them too much," he said.

We finished the meal, cleaned up, went outside together. Mouse, too.

Osh handed me a bushel basket and, armed with a pitchfork, began to harvest seaweed from the wrack line.

When the basket was full, we each took a handle and lugged

it up to the high rocks where we spread it to wait for rain. When it was washed and dried, we'd hoe it into the garden, food for our food.

Osh began on a second basket while I thought about whether I was brave enough to cross to New Bedford alone. I was a good sailor, but I knew that even a skiff could be a lot to handle in a strong wind, crosscurrents, shipping lanes.

If I went, I would have to take the ferry.

"I haven't been to New Bedford since before I came here," Osh said, as if he could read my mind. "And I have no desire to go back there. Ever. Full of whale stink. Everything too fast. Too crowded." He ripped an old conch shell off a hank of dead man's fingers and tossed it aside. "I'm sorry, Crow, but I just can't go there."

I didn't want to cause Osh grief. But I did not see why I had to choose between him and a brother who might be just nine miles away.

"If Miss Maggie goes with me, can I go?" I said.

"And how will you pay for the passage?"

This, as nothing else, gave me pause. Everything that belonged to Osh belonged to me as well. The money he earned from cutting ice or trapping lobsters or painting his pictures went for things we couldn't grow ourselves. But if I ever needed anything from the mainland, he sent for it with no fuss at all: pencils for my lessons, a new pair of winter boots when I outgrew the last, a new book now and then, medicine that Miss Maggie could not concoct on her own.

"Will you not pay for my passage?" I asked him in a small voice.

Osh stuck his pitchfork in the sand and ran his hands through his hair. He looked at me steadily, his mouth tight. "If you insist on going, I will give you the fare," he said. He paused. "And tell Miss Maggie thank you for taking my place."

When I went looking for her, I found Miss Maggie coming up the lane from the post office, on her way home.

"Not tomorrow," she said when I asked if she would go to New Bedford with me. "Cinders has come up lame and I need to stay with her. But maybe in a few days, when she's better, if Osh will go with us."

But I knew he would not.

And I didn't want to wait a few days.

"Maybe in a few days then," I said, turning back toward home. "I hope Cinders feels better."

As I walked past the bass stands and across the low channel to our beach, I decided that I would take the ferry to New Bedford alone.

I was twelve years old.

I could sail a skiff, wrangle a lobster, save a birdman from starving to death.

Surely I could ride a ferry to the city and back again.

"There's weather coming," Osh said when I woke the next morning. "You may have a wet crossing home from the city." I walked outside and blinked at the blue sky, sheer yellow sunlight, small breeze.

Osh was usually right about the weather, but not always.

"Don't worry. We'll be fine. And I'll tell Miss Maggie to bring a rain bonnet, just in case," I said, taking the bowl of oatmeal he offered. He had crumbled some crisp bacon on top, which was unusual. So was the mug of coffee he set next to me at the table. I usually had to beg him for a cup.

When he poured in some cream, I was more surprised, still.

"I'll fix you a pocket lunch," he said, which he'd done before, when I went to help Miss Maggie find her sheep scattered wide across the island. An apple for one pocket. A roll stuffed with cheese and jerky for another, my body warming it into softness as I worked.

"Thank you," I said as I bent to my breakfast, sad about deceiving him. Better that, though, than pushing him to go to New Bedford with me.

Nobody strands himself on an island unless he's finished with the mainland.

An hour later, I waited on the sand while the ferry passengers crossed the long boardwalk from the pier to dry ground. Lots of people had come for a holiday, a good shore dinner, and then home by dark. Ladies in white dresses. Men in summer suits.

I watched them parade off the boardwalk and up the lane. Some of them looked at me curiously. One woman even said hello. And then they were gone, and the boardwalk free for those of us outward bound.

I followed a few other islanders along the boardwalk toward the steamship. I knew them and they knew me, but no one said very much.

At the gangway, the mate took my money, same as theirs. To him, I was just a skinny kid. I smiled on my way forward to the bow.

The breeze was strengthening as we pulled away from the pier. In the distance, mare's tails swept out of nowhere across the sky. They were often the first sign of a storm, the frayed hem of cloud heavy with weather. But they were a long way off, and the sky overhead was still a spotless blue as we steamed west.

At some point, I realized I was in unfamiliar waters, closer to the continent than the islands. Traveling by steam instead of by sail was odd, too. We went straight, regardless of the wind, at a steady speed, cutting through the waves instead of riding them, with but one purpose: to get there. Which suited me fine that morning. I was anxious to reach the city.

But, as it turned out, I discovered something before we ever made land.

As we neared the mouth of New Bedford Harbor, a schooner flying a long green streamer off its mainmast, its sails plump, its bow rising and dipping, came out through the channel toward us. We gave way a little, as all engine ships must to those under sail, but we passed close by, and I could see the sailors clearly. They were lined up at the rail, filling themselves with the sight of the home they might not see again for weeks. Maybe months.

One of them looked like me.

He was near the bow of his ship, I in the bow of the ferry, and for a long moment we were directly across from each other, staring.

"Jason?" I called, but there was wind, and I could tell that he hadn't heard me. He cupped a hand behind one ear and leaned over the rail as far as he could, and I yelled again, more loudly, "Jason!"

But I still couldn't be sure that he'd heard me.

Without unlocking my eyes from his, I moved toward the stern, and he did the same as the two boats passed alongside each other, so for a minute—no more—we stayed as close as we could. And then, from the stern of the ferry, I stood and watched him in the stern of the schooner, the distance between us lengthening, and I waved.

The sailor who looked like me waved back, but so did all the others lined up along the stern, nothing more than friendly.

And then the ferry steamed into the harbor, the schooner tacked away, and the sailor was just a man.

"The *Shearwater*," I said aloud, so I would remember the name of that schooner and know it when it returned.

I didn't move from that spot until I could no longer see the ship at all.

Perhaps he was nothing to me. A stranger by now busy with the rigging, all of his thoughts tuned to the sea. How he looked, nothing more than a coincidence. How he looked, nothing more than something I wanted to see.

Or perhaps he was still standing by the rail of the *Shearwater*, wondering about me. Perhaps even, like me, filled with an odd warmth that didn't weaken as he sailed away.

Chapter 21

When the ferry tied up at the dock, I was tempted to stay on board and wait for the return trip. The sight of that sailor who looked so much like me might be a better answer than anything I would find in New Bedford. But the answer I wanted and the one I needed were two different things. I would do what I had come to do.

Now that I had reached the city, though, I was no longer so eager for it.

Osh had been right. Even before I stepped foot onshore, I was startled by the place. It reeked of whale and waste. All along the dock, there were vast pens of barrels covered with seaweed and hundreds of bales of cotton waiting for the mills. Men everywhere, of every color, stripped to the waist, labored in the sun. Horses worked alongside engines alongside people alongside a harbor afloat with trash and oil. In the distance, factories smoked their pipes. Past the docks: tall buildings and long straight streets. Miss Maggie had told me about automobiles, and I had seen some pictures of them, but the ones I saw here—their fumes and rumble, the blare of their horns—amazed me. I didn't see a tree anywhere.

"You comin'?" a deckhand called to me, and I realized I was the only passenger still aboard.

"I am," I said, hurrying past him and down the gangway onto the dock, where I stopped short.

Nothing so far had alarmed me as much as the sight of a black dog, boils riding its back like a second spine, a rat as big as Mouse clenched in its teeth. No one else gave it a second look.

I didn't know where I was going, so I simply went. I hurried to catch up with the other islanders who had come for business of their own.

"Hey," I called to one of them, a farmer, Mr. Cook.

He turned. "Off on another grand adventure, are you, Crow? Saving the bird keeper wasn't enough for you?"

"Do you know where the orphanage is?" I asked him.

"Ain't no orphanage in New Bedford," he said. "Not anymore."

And I cursed myself for thinking I could do this without any planning whatsoever. The city felt like a fortress, huge and unfriendly. And I had never felt so small.

"But where it was— that's still there," he said, and I took hope.

"What do you mean?"

"Brought my mother here when she took sick. To the hospital.

And just by there is the old building used to be the orphanage. Part of St. Luke's now." He pointed away from the docks. "Go on up Union, left on County, right on Allen. And be quick, Crow. It's a long walk. And there's but one ferry back to Cuttyhunk today."

It felt odd to be wearing shoes in June, but I was glad to have them since the streets were sharp with bits of glass and metal, filthy with dust and dreck. Everyone walked so quickly here, nobody saying much to anyone else, all around them a cloud of commotion. The windows of the shops were full of things I couldn't imagine ever having, and the reflection of the passersby and the street full of cars made those glimpses of another life seem distant and insubstantial, like dreams.

I watched for County, crossed Union to get to it, dodging cars and trucks that honked at me, watched for Allen, crossed again, more carefully, and took it straight up, block after block, looking for St. Luke's.

I was hot and sticky, my feet hurt, I wanted just one tree and a small patch of shade—or the ocean, better yet—and I was hungry for my pocket lunch. Too early, though, to eat what I had or I'd have nothing left when I needed it most.

And suddenly I was at the hospital. There was no mistaking it. It was huge and beautiful in its own way.

I felt like a stranger, a sore thumb among all these city people, but no one paid the least bit of attention to me as I climbed the stairs and ducked through the big doors of St. Luke's.

Here was a city within a city. Bustle and clatter. Sour smells overlaid with alcohol fumes. Loud shoes and, somewhere, a woman crying. And I had too many choices and no idea how to make one. A rising sense that I was on a fool's errand. Until a young woman at the front desk said, "Can I help you?" She motioned me closer, curiosity plain on her face. "Are you lost?"

"No, but I've never been to the city before. I'm looking for what used to be the orphanage," I said. Then quickly corrected myself: "Really, someone who can tell me about a boy who used to live there."

The woman examined me some more, quizzical, not quite smiling. "Well, any child who ever lived there hasn't for years," she said.

I nodded. "I didn't expect to find him," I said. "Just someone who could tell me about him."

"I haven't worked here long enough to help you," she said, "but there are a few people in the wards who've been here since then."

She gave me directions to the nursery. "You'll find Mrs. Pelham there," she said. "She helps with the babies now, but she used to work in the orphanage. Start with her. If anyone can answer your questions, she can."

I made my way through a maze of corridors, out through a door into a yard with, finally, trees, across the yard and the street beyond and up the walkway to the steps of another building, not as big as St. Luke's proper, through the door, down a corridor, and up a flight of stairs to a ward where I could hear babies crying.

"Can I help you?" asked a nurse coming out of the nursery just as I meant to go in. Her uniform was so white it made my eyes hurt.

"I've come to see Mrs. Pelham," I said, trying not to sound as uncertain as I felt.

"Well, you can't go in there," she said, looking me up and down as if I had fleas, "but I'll see if she can come out here for a minute. What's your name?"

"Crow," I said.

She frowned at me. "Like the bird?"

"Like the bird," I said.

She raised one eyebrow but went into the nursery and, moments later, returned with an older woman in tow.

"This is Mrs. Pelham," she said, and then swept off down the hallway like a great white goose.

Mrs. Pelham's face was old but she moved like someone younger, and when she smiled I could see that her teeth were still strong. I wondered what had mapped her face like that.

She peered at me, her brow furrowed. "Do I know you?"

"No," I said.

"Then what can I do for you?" she said.

"They told me you used to work in the orphanage."

She nodded. "Yes I did. For years."

I hadn't expected such luck. "I'm trying to find out about a boy who used to live there. His name is Jason. He came from Penikese Island when he was just a new baby. Did you know him?"

Mrs. Pelham stood up straighter. She wasn't much taller than I was, but she suddenly seemed formidable. And every trace of curiosity in her eyes was suddenly gone, replaced with something else.

"You're here about Jason?" she said. She looked not angry, quite, but serious.

I nodded.

"This ward is for mothers and their babies," she said. "But it used to be where the orphans lived."

It was not a bad place. The corridors were wide, the ceilings high. It was clean with lots of windows.

But it was not a home.

As I stood there, I thought of the cottage that Osh had built. So small. So crooked. The sound of rain on its roof. The sight of Osh stirring the fire. The amber light it made. The shadows flitting on the walls.

"Did Jason live here?"

She pointed. "In the room at the end, there."

"By himself?"

She sighed. "Why do you want to know about him?"

"I live on one of the other Elizabeths," I said. "By Cuttyhunk. And I think . . . I wonder . . ." I wasn't sure how to make my long story short enough. "It's possible that I have a brother named Jason who was sent here. And I'm trying to find out what happened to him."

Suddenly, as if I had said something warm and kind,

everything stern about her softened. She closed her eyes. Her lips trembled. She backed toward a bench and sat down, her hands in fists beneath her chin, head bowed. *"Oh my,"* she whispered. *"Oh my."*

I sat beside her, and when she didn't move away I liked her very much.

"Mrs. Pelham?" I said. "Are you all right?"

She opened her eyes and nodded. "I am," she said. Her hands fell into her lap. She turned to me and smiled a little. "It's just that we all gave up hope of ever finding a family for Jason. And now a family has come to find him."

Chapter 22

*I*t was odd to think that I—just me, one person—was a family. And that I really might have a brother.

"Do you know where Jason is now?" I asked.

Mrs. Pelham shook her head. "Not anymore," she said. "The orphanage stopped taking in children when Jason was five years old. All the orphans were placed out, with foster families. Except him." Her lips trembled again, a little. "You know about Penikese, then? And why he was sent here?"

I nodded.

"The poor boy. The doctors here told us to consider him contagious until they were sure he didn't have leprosy. So we kept the other children away, and we wore gloves and masks for the first few months. And even after that we kept our distance, though I found that hard to do. We would bathe him, of course, and dress him and do all the other things he needed us to do when he was very small, but he was alone too much. Such a sweet, quiet, big-eyed baby."

She shook her head. "After the first couple of years, when I was convinced he wasn't sick, they said I could hold him, but he wouldn't let me. He acted like it hurt to be touched." She began to cry but didn't make any fuss about it. "He didn't talk, either, or sing or play or seem interested in much. Just looked out the window for hours, sometimes hummed a little. When he slept, I would sit by his bed and stroke his little arm or lay my hand on his forehead, just so some part of him would know that he wasn't alone."

"But what happened to him when all the other children left?"

Mrs. Pelham wiped her cheeks with her sleeves. "We kept him here. What else could we do? I couldn't take him home with me." She looked away. "My husband is a good man, but he wouldn't have it. We had children of our own."

"So he stayed in the orphanage?"

"In that same room, yes, but he had the run of the place, too, as he got older. And that's when he began to talk." She rubbed her eyes with the heels of her hands. "To the patients at first. I was shocked, I can tell you, to find him sitting on the foot of a bed one day, talking to a little girl who had been hurt in a grease fire. She was burned on her legs, where the fire had climbed up her skirt before her mother put it out. And there was Jason, asking what was wrong with her. I remember it so well. I remember her saying, 'I got burned in a fire,' and him saying, 'Does it hurt?'"

She looked at me, clearly amazed still after all this time. "Five years old before he said a word . . . and then talking like you and me. I couldn't get over it. It was as if he'd decided to just get on with it. Just start from there and make his own way. *At five*. And he did, too. Never did learn to read or write, though we tried to teach him. Never did spend much time again in that room. He slept wherever there was a spare bed, went down to the kitchens when he was hungry, kept himself clean enough and dressed and busy helping out in the wards. Fetching and carrying. Showing people the way. And then, when he was just a little older, adventuring around the city on his own, though I tried to keep him close." She laughed. "Which was like trying to keep a cat close. Quite impossible."

I tried to picture it: a child half my age, earning his keep, roaming the city, his home wherever he was at the moment, his life entirely in his own hands.

I had thought of myself as a resourceful person, but not compared to him.

"Is he still around here?" I asked, though I knew he was perhaps twenty by now and surely long gone from St. Luke's.

"I do wish he were," she said. "And he does show up from time to time. Once with a valentine he'd made out of shells." She rubbed her eyes again. "Until then, I didn't think he cared much for me, and who could blame him? Someone who's supposed to look after orphans, too afraid to care for him properly. Or to take him in when he needed a home. But he seemed to understand, as he got older, that nothing is quite as simple as it seems."

"He brought you a sailor's valentine?" I pictured the young man on the *Shearwater*. "Did he go to sea?"

She nodded. "How did you know?"

I stood up. "When I came in on the ferry from Cuttyhunk, I saw a sailor on a schooner. The *Shearwater*. He looked just like me."

Mrs. Pelham smiled. "I doubt very much that he was Jason," she said. "I haven't seen him for years. But you do look almost like he did when he was your age."

We talked for a little while longer, and then I decided I ought to head for the ferry dock.

"When Jason comes back to see you again, will you tell him about me?"

"I will," she said. "A girl named Crow. If he comes back."

"From over by Cuttyhunk."

"From over by Cuttyhunk. I won't forget. How could I?" she said. "It's not often I get a second chance like this one."

I walked back to the docks so deep in thought that I nearly fell through an open cellar hatch in the sidewalk. A man rolling a barrel from a truck yelled, "Hey there!" at the last second, and I pulled up short, sidestepped the gap, and went on my way.

I knew there was a movie house in New Bedford. Miss Maggie had told me about motion pictures, and I'd always wanted to see one. I knew there were confectioners there, too, who sold candies I'd always wanted to taste. But even if I'd had the money for such things—which I didn't—I would not have spent a moment on them.

I could not imagine a movie more interesting than this day of mine, or a candy as sweet as the idea that Jason was real and might be my brother.

I kept telling myself to add the *might* when I thought about that.

Until I knew for certain, *might* was important.

But Mrs. Pelham had said I looked like Jason had at my age. That was real.

And so was the sailor I'd seen on the *Shearwater*. Whether he was Jason or not, he was a place to start.

I would watch for the *Shearwater* to come through the Graveyard. And I would be patient. Or at least I would try.

As I made my way through the noisy, crowded, dirty streets, I remembered what Osh had said about New Bedford making me dissatisfied with our island. With our life there.

But all I wanted right then was to go home.

Chapter 23

When I reached the dock, the ferry wasn't there.

"Gone for a run to Mattapoisett," the dockmaster said through his wild beard, his long pipe clenched in his brown teeth. "Back soon."

"And when does it leave for Cuttyhunk?" I asked, squinting up at him. The sun, behind his head, gave him a halo, but he smelled awful, like old fish and old man, both of which needed a bath.

"Seven bells," he said. "Half past three, give or take."

"What time is it now?"

He glanced over his shoulder at the sun. "Just two," he said. "Four bells. You've got some waiting to do."

As I turned to be on my way, a thought occurred to me. "Do you know a schooner called the *Shearwater*?" I asked him.

"I do," he said. "A scow lucky to be afloat."

"Do you know where she was bound?"

He squinted, his mouth pursed. "Maine, I reckon," he said after a moment. "Portland. Not sure where she's headed after that."

"If she comes straight back from Portland, how long will that take?"

He cast an eye skyward. "With enough wind, not too much, up and back?" He did some figuring. "A week? Maybe more. But if they were bound somewhere else after Portland? Months, maybe." At which he shrugged, his pipe bobbing in his teeth. "Could be anywhere and back anytime," he said. "Best I can tell you."

And he hobbled away, yelling something at a deckhand who was dumping slops off the stern of a sloop at anchor. Baitfish below swarmed madly among the potato peels and eggshells floating on the water.

I turned away and found a perch on a pylon where a herring gull had been keeping watch but was now down among the baitfish, guzzling its lunch.

I ate my own, one pocket at a time, until I'd finished the stuffed roll and the apple, which was juicy enough to be both food and drink. I felt better. Not hungry. Not thirsty. Just hot in the midday sun, anxious to be out of my shoes, eager to be on the islands again.

But then I glanced down the dock toward the street and grew

cold all at once, then again hot, at the sight of the man from Penikese, the big man who had left Mr. Sloan for dead, coming out of a doorway.

He stopped, looking carefully right and left, and I memorized him as he was now. His brown trousers, black shirt, brown hat with a rolled brim.

After one more look in both directions, he walked off along the waterfront out of sight.

I hadn't expected to see him here. Surely he'd known someone would find Mr. Sloan sooner or later and come looking for the man who'd held him prisoner.

Perhaps he thought Mr. Sloan had died by now. Perhaps he wasn't worried that we'd seen him on Penikese. After all, he didn't know that Mr. Sloan had lived to tell his tale of captivity and abuse. And he didn't know that Osh would draw a picture to help the police hunt for him.

But why stay so close by? Why take the chance?

I thought about following him. I thought about staying where it was safe.

I thought about Mr. Sloan sitting in the sand, scrubbing himself clean.

And I headed off to follow the man before I could think another thing.

He had a good head start, but I was quick, and he was big enough to stand out.

Up ahead I could see him striding along with a clear purpose, a good head taller than anyone else on the street. Even when I had no clear sight line, I could see his brown hat bobbing above the crowd, and I kept my eyes on it as I followed, ready at any moment to duck into an alleyway if he happened to turn around.

But he didn't. And I stayed close enough so that when he opened a shop door and disappeared inside, I had time to slow and creep up to the shop.

The window was full of jewelry and guns. A long fur coat. Gold pocket watches. A gleaming saddle and a silver platter carved all over with scrollwork.

I scampered across the street to a shed on the docks and ducked behind it to wait until he reappeared. The empty corpse of a pigeon lay at my feet. Cigar butts and rotten seaweed, too. Things I couldn't name, all of it steeped in old rainwater and mud.

To my relief, the shop door opened again soon enough, and the big man came out. He looked furious, even from a distance. Bunched up like a watchdog. And I ducked back out of sight to wait until he'd left.

When I looked again, I saw him headed back the way he'd come, and I knew I'd have to be careful not to run into him again when I returned to the ferry dock.

From my post on the wharf, I could see the sign above the shop. PAWNBROKER, it said. I didn't know what that meant.

I crossed the street.

A bell jangled when I opened the door and went inside. The place was filled with treasures of every kind. Big glass cases of jewelry and guns. Along one wall, fur coats hung, empty and bored. On another, beautiful paintings. Shelves filled with lace fans, crystal, cigarette lighters, and perfume bottles. A barrel bristled with canes, some with ivory handles.

At the end of the shop, behind a jewelry case, a man in a visor looked up from his work and said, "What do you want?" without a trace of welcome.

"Just to know what a pawnbroker is," I said in a small voice.

Which drew an unexpected smile.

"You bring me things worth money, I pay you a fee. If you return soon enough, you can buy your belongings back for a bigger fee. If not, I get to sell them to someone else. You got something to pawn?"

I went closer. On the case in front of him was a square of black cloth. Laid out on it was a pretty necklace, gold, with a locket shaped like a heart.

"I might," I said, but I didn't think he would give me anything for my shoes.

He grinned. "Had your hand in somebody's pocket, did you?"

Which set me back a step. "Not me," I said. "But I'll bet that man who was just in here stole that necklace."

He didn't like that.

His face changed. He made as if to come around the counter, and I turned and fled out the door and down the street at such a run that I nearly caught up to the big man I'd been tracking.

He had stopped to buy a sausage from a cart alongside the curb near the ferry dock.

My face was the only thing about me he might recognize, so I slipped past him and straight along to the dock, never looking back except to glance quickly, for trucks, before crossing to where the ferry would tie up, and soon I hoped.

From there, I couldn't see the man, but I went, regardless, as far down the dock as I could to wait for the ferry. There was nowhere to hide here. But I was small, the world was big, and if I was still and quiet I could be invisible, as much a part of the dock as the pylons or the gulls that perched on them, watching everything with their flat yellow eyes.

I watched, too, and never let down my guard for a moment until the ferry steamed again into port and it was time to board.

But as I stood in line at the gangway, I forgot to be so careful, and when I glanced again down the dock I saw him there, standing square and tense, looking right at me.

His face was a confusion of anger and surprise. Mine, I imagined, was one-hundred-percent fear.

But he stayed where he was, watching, until it was my turn to board.

By the time I made my way to the bow to look for him, he was gone.

As before, there were only a few of us on the crossing, and there was plenty of room for me to sit by myself and let my thoughts sort themselves out.

I was still as tense as an anchor rope in a current, and my

mind churned with all I'd done and seen; but the farther we traveled, the more New Bedford seemed like another world, far away, that couldn't touch me now. Not even the terrible man who was still somewhere over there, perhaps at this very moment on his way out of town, as spooked by the sight of me as I'd been by him.

And I convinced myself that I would never see him again.

Chapter 24

Osh was waiting for me when the ferry docked.

I saw him watching from the beach as I walked along the boardwalk with the handful of islanders coming home.

He didn't say a word when I joined him, but he put his hand on my shoulder and kept it there for a long moment.

"Don't ever do that to me again," he said quietly. He sounded as if there were a fire in his chest and he was doing everything possible to contain it.

"I'm sorry," I said, and I was.

"You'll need to say that to Miss Maggie, too," he said. "She nearly swam over to New Bedford when we figured out you'd gone there alone."

"But not you?"

He gave me a warning look. "You want to go off on your own, go ahead. But you should know that any harm that comes to you comes to me, too. And Miss Maggie. Real harm. Do you understand?"

I nodded. "I'm sorry," I said again. I sat down in the grass along the edge of the lane and took off my shoes. "I hated the city," I said.

He sighed. "Good."

I tied my shoes together and carried them by their laces as we headed up the lane toward Miss Maggie's.

We found her in the barn, which was hot and hazy with straw dust and pollen. She was on her knees alongside Cinders, feeling one of her fetlocks for heat, when Osh and I stopped at the open door to the stall.

She climbed to her feet. I was used to some thunder in her face, but I'd never seen it so full of storm. "You will never do that again," she said. It wasn't a question.

"No, I won't," I said. "I'm sorry."

"And using me like you did. Lying that I would be with you. What were you thinking?"

I shook my head. "I needed to go to New Bedford. To look for Jason. I'm sorry that I didn't wait until you could go with me."

Miss Maggie came out with us and shut the door to the stall behind her. "So am I," she said. "Now come along. Osh and I were too scared to eat, and I, for one, am starving."

I hadn't expected a Miss Maggie supper, and I was glad I hadn't eaten much that day, but I wasn't glad when she turned aside my offer to help in the kitchen. "No, go on and wait," she said. "I'd just as soon do it myself."

So Osh and I sat outside, at the trestle table in the shade of her hornbeam tree, while Miss Maggie made our supper. Above us, a nest full of young crows cawed for theirs, too. I could see them leaning far out into the open air, hours from flight.

"Why is that nest so high up?" I said. "What if the babies fall when they try to fly?"

Osh tipped his head back and peered through the branches. "More than one answer to that," he said.

"Like what?"

"They build it high up so it's harder for hunters to get there."

"What about other birds? Doesn't a high-up nest make it easier for a hawk to get a baby crow?"

Osh shrugged. "They have to build their nest somewhere."

"And what's the point of building it high up anyway if the babies fall and break their necks when they try to fly?"

Osh shook his head. "They don't try until they're ready."

An answer that made my brain hurt. "But how do they know they can fly if they haven't flown yet?"

"I suspect they pay attention to what they know." As he had told me I should.

We looked long at each other, and I saw him soften a bit. "They're the ones who know best when they're ready to fly," he said. He leaned close and took my hand. "But they don't lie about it. And they don't sneak off like you did."

His hand was terribly rough and hard, but he held mine as if I were made of petals.

"I won't do it again," I said. "Next time, I'll tell you."

I expected him to argue about the *Next time*, but he didn't. Instead, he nodded. And I was both happy and sad about that.

Perhaps that was how those young crows felt as they nestled in their warm and sturdy nest, yearning for the sky.

Miss Maggie gave us lobster cakes, biscuits, and cool water with sprigs of mint.

"You'll eat first and then you'll tell us every bit of it," she said, sitting at one end of the table, Osh at the other.

None of us said much as we ate. It was that good.

The lobster cakes were hot and buttery, brown and crunchy on the outside, sweet and white on the inside. She'd baked cheese into the biscuits and topped each one with a dab of pepper relish. For dessert, she brought out a dish of strawberries dusted with a little cane sugar.

The breeze curtsied as it passed by.

A chimney swift sketched a curlicue overhead.

If there had been music, it might have been too much to bear.

"I like it here better than in the city," I said to Osh.

"Of course you do," Miss Maggie said.

And then I told them about my day. Starting with the sailor

who looked like me. Ending with the big man and the pawn-broker and how he'd seen me on the docks.

Miss Maggie interjected now and then, as was her habit, but Osh listened carefully until I was through.

"Not a wild-goose chase, then," he said.

"No," I said. "The Jason from Penikese might still be around here, somewhere. Maybe even that sailor I saw. And Mrs. Pelham said I do look like him. So now I just need to know if I am that other baby. The one who didn't really die."

We all thought about that for a moment.

"The letter from the nurse might tell you if you're that baby," Miss Maggie said. "It should be here any day now."

"Good," Osh said. "And then all this will be done."

"With that terrible man just across the water?" Miss Maggie said. "We need to send another message to those police officers."

"And you are just the one to send it," Osh told her. "But you," he said to me. "Will it be enough for you to know where you came from and how to find your brother, if you have one?"

"I'm not sure," I said slowly. "There's still that ring. That letter that came with it. This . . ." I touched the feather on my cheek. "The lambs in the graveyard and in the cottage." I couldn't understand the impatience on his face. "I'll bet you know a lot about your own history, Osh. What's wrong with wanting to know mine?"

"My history is done and gone and better left that way," he said. He stood up and carried the empty platters toward the house.

"I can't believe he doesn't want to know about his family," I said as we watched him walk toward the house. "Whether they're all right. Where they are now."

She looked at me with a sad little smile. "He knows everything he needs to know," she said. "You're right here."

Chapter 25

*T*he next morning, as Osh and I worked dried seaweed into our garden, Miss Maggie appeared by the bass stands.

"Your letter came," she called as she crossed the mid-tide channel, her skirts held high in one hand, her shoes and a white envelope in the other. "From the Penikese nurse. Miss Morgan."

"We're almost done here," Osh said, so I worked on, faster than before, while Miss Maggie found a seat on the rocks and spread her skirts to dry.

"Oh, for the love of Pete," she said after a bit. "That seaweed's not going to run off if you stop for just a minute, Daniel."

But he didn't stop until we'd tucked every last shred of seaweed underground where it could do its work.

As soon as we were done, Mouse crept out of the grasses and

attacked a small hole in the soil, dragging out a strand of sea lettuce so she could properly subdue it. But the sea lettuce did not
put up much of a fight, and after a moment Mouse decided to
attack Osh's bootlaces instead, rolling in the dirt until he lifted
her up and tossed her gently aside.

I leaned my hoe against the rocks and went to sit with Miss
Maggie. Osh stayed where he was.

She handed me the letter and watched as I opened the envelope carefully and unfolded the paper inside.

I read it aloud to them both.

> *Dear Crow,* it began.
>
> *I hope you can forgive me for being cautious. You
> sound like an honest person looking for answers, but I have
> learned that not everything is as it seems. And not everyone
> can be trusted.*

I made a face at Miss Maggie. "What's she talking about?"
"Keep reading," she said.

> *When Dr. Eastman showed me your first letter, I
> wanted to take the next train north to see you for myself.
> How else could I know for sure who had written that
> letter? And how can I know who wrote the second letter,
> the one that came to me directly, with that mysterious list
> of words?*

I remembered writing that letter, not trusting the nurse enough, afraid to spell out what I wanted to know. And now here she was, likewise suspicious.

It may seem odd, I read, *to be so careful, but I have reasons. The main one: a man I met here in Louisiana. A workman who had come to repair the roof on the hospital. Mr. Kendall. Mr. James Kendall. One day he asked me about a necklace I was wearing. Asked me if it was real— real gold, a real ruby in the pendant.*

He was charming about it. Said that it was very pretty but not nearly as pretty as I was.

I was flattered. I admit it. I am not and never have been pretty. But it was nice to think that I was. And I told him, yes, the necklace was made from real gold. A real ruby. I told him that it had been a gift from my friend Susanna, a patient I'd treated on Penikese Island. At the leper colony there.

I expected him to back away, like everyone else did, but he didn't.

And when I explained that she had found it while digging for cinquefoil root—which we used on open sores—he seemed quite interested.

He asked me if I would like to have dinner with him some time, and I said yes.

We went out together just a day later. It was so nice for

someone to be unafraid of me. Most everyone else kept me at arm's length. But not him.

And here I stopped again, this time to consider what I hadn't realized before—that the people who cared for lepers took more than one kind of risk.

"Crow?" Miss Maggie said, and I returned to the letter.

And Mr. Kendall listened to me! I read. *No one had ever listened to me the way he listened to me.*

He asked me a lot of questions about Penikese and the leper colony and my friend Susanna.

I told him, and I am telling you now, that although she'd been savaged by her awful disease, she was a beautiful woman. Kind. Sweet. So smart.

I told him all about her and our friendship. How brave she was. How hard she worked to help the other patients, no matter how much she herself was ailing.

And I answered his questions about life on that island.

I thought he was my friend.

But soon after that, the necklace went missing from my room at the hospital, and the man disappeared, too.

What a fool I was.

I can't be sure that he took it.

I also can't be sure that you aren't that man, writing to see if I know anything more about all this.

*In fact, I do know more. But I won't put it into a
letter.*

*If you are, indeed, that terrible man, then shame
on you.*

*If not, these words I have written in response to the
ones you sent me should mean quite a lot. I hope so.*

On the second page, Nurse Evelyn had written my list of
words and, next to each one of them, something of her own.

I held the page out so Miss Maggie could see it, too. But I
read it aloud for Osh to hear.

Baby, I had written.

You, she had replied.

For *Skiff*, she had written, *It was an old one that no one missed
for weeks. And then I told Dr. Eastman that it had drifted away on
the tide.*

Next to *Ring*, a line that made my heart hurt: *Susanna wore
this.* And then, something more mysterious. *It is your inheritance.
I think there may be more.*

"What's an inheritance?" I asked Miss Maggie.

"It's what someone leaves behind when she dies," she said.
"A gift."

For *Little feather*, Nurse Evelyn had written: *The mark by
which I would know that you are hers.*

And for *Lambs*: *Another way you'll know what she wanted you
to know.*

And finally, *Bright sea.*

My name, she had written. *Morgan. Which is Celtic, like me. It means "bright sea." And your mother gave it to you, too. Which was also her gift to me, better than the necklace.*

After that, Nurse Evelyn had written, *Someday, I hope to take that train north to look for you.*

And she had signed it,

Evelyn Morgan

But below that was a postscript. And it, too, helped answer a question I'd been asking myself.

> *If you are who I think you are,* she wrote, *I hope you will forgive me if I've made mistakes. Not long after you were born, someone sent a letter to Penikese, asking questions about a baby who had washed up on one of the Elizabeths. I fetched the mail that day. The letter wasn't addressed to anyone in particular. Just the hospital. So I opened it. And I burned it. Susanna and your father had chosen to give you a chance at something other than Penikese or an orphanage, and that letter meant you had arrived safely in a better place. That was all Susanna wanted. So that's what I gave her.*

I folded up the letter and tucked it back inside the envelope.

"Susanna was my mother," I said.

Miss Maggie nodded. "She was."

"And now I know for sure that I do have a brother, whether he's that sailor or not."

"Yes, you do," she said.

"And Elvan is my father," I said. "Or was."

At which Osh put aside his hoe and went into the house.

Miss Maggie followed him. And I followed her, Mouse at my heels.

Chapter 26

Osh went straight to his easel, where he'd been working on a painting of Mouse curled up in a lightship basket, her tail hanging over the rim.

I once asked him why he'd never painted my portrait. He said, "I have. Over and over again. Every time I paint the sea."

At the time, that answer—the idea that I'd come from the sea, that I was like the sea—had made me feel strong and unusual. And I still loved that answer. But it was not the only true thing about me.

"You're upset, aren't you, Osh?" I said. "Because I said Elvan was my father. But he was. That doesn't have anything to do with you."

He put down his brush and turned to me. "You're right, it doesn't," he said. "And I'm glad that you know what you wanted to know."

"So am I," I said. "I'm not surprised to know they were my parents. I've learned that, bit by bit, for a while. But now that I know for sure, all of it, I feel . . . like I make more sense than I did before." I frowned at the look on his face. "Is there something wrong with that?"

Osh sighed. "You've always made sense to me."

"You've known me longer than I've known myself," I said.

Osh nodded. "So are you finally done now that you know what you wanted to know?"

I shook my head slowly. "I mean to go out there again. To Penikese."

Osh turned back to his painting. "To look for your inheritance? So you can buy things I can't buy for you?"

But that wasn't it. "No, and you know that's not what I want."

I went outside and sat in the sand by the door. Mouse came to join me. She climbed in my lap and rubbed her chin against mine. Her claws always came out when she was happy, and I knew I'd have tiny red wounds from how she was kneading me, purring, her eyes looking earnestly into mine.

I could hear what Miss Maggie was saying. She was angry, which made her loud.

"That was cruel, Daniel. You know better than that."

A pause. Then, "Why do you call me Daniel?"

Again, a pause.

"What does that have to do with anything?"

I heard the scrape of his chair as he stood up. "In all the

years I've known you, you've never asked me my name. You just decided to call me Daniel."

"First of all," she said, "I most certainly did ask you your name. When you came here, I called over to you. I called over to you again and again, and you never told me your name." She paused. "Would you prefer that I call you Osh?"

"Osh is what Crow calls me."

I pushed Mouse gently off my lap and stood up, into the doorway. They both looked at me.

"Why are you talking about this?" I asked him.

"I'm beginning to think we should start over again," he said. "I'll call you Morgan from now on. And you can call me something else, too. Something better than Osh."

And he walked out of the house.

I looked at Miss Maggie and she at me.

"His name is Osh," I said, and I could hear the tears in my throat.

"I know," she said, putting her arms around me. "He'll come around. He's just . . . well, I don't know. Maybe lonely for the ways things were."

"The way they still are," I said. "Nothing has changed. He's still Osh."

"But are you still Crow?" she asked. "Or are you Morgan now?"

"I'm Crow," I said. "I'm Crow, and he's Osh."

"Then go tell him that," she said.

I found him behind the house, at the cistern, filling a pitcher for the house. He looked up, saw me, closed the spigot, and set the pitcher in the sand.

"I'm sorry," he said, holding out a hand to me.

I took it, and he pulled me to him for a moment, his other hand in my hair.

"I don't understand," I said into his shirt. "Can I not call you Osh anymore?"

He turned me loose and took hold of my chin, tipping my head back, looking straight into my face.

"Always, you can," he said. "Always, you can. And I am going to call you Crow no matter what."

"Well, good," I said shakily. "Otherwise, I won't have any name at all."

He straightened up. "Not Morgan?"

"Not Morgan," I said. I picked up the pitcher in both hands and hugged it to my chest. "The mother who gave me that name is gone. I never knew any other father. You are here," I said. "You, I know."

He nodded once. "Morgan can be your name, too, after Crow."

"Maybe," I said. "We'll see."

We went around the house and through the door together.

Miss Maggie was waiting for us in a chair by the fireplace. Her eyes were red.

"So what am *I* supposed to call you?" she said to Osh. She

sounded more sad than angry, though some of both. "Or would you rather I just went away?"

I put the pitcher on the table and watched the next part of this strange day. Miss Maggie, forlorn as a cold lamb. Osh, looking like he had a bellyache.

"No, I would not," he said.

"Then tell me what to call you, or I won't call you anything at all." She stood up and tried to look fierce.

After a moment, he said his name. His whole name. *Osh* was only one part of it. He blurted this out like it had been sitting in the back of his throat for years.

Miss Maggie looked up at him from under her brows. "Is that your name?" she asked.

He nodded. He said it again.

"Why are you telling me now, after all this time?" she asked.

He looked at his hands, at the floor, at the wall above her head. "My name is important," he said. "I don't tell it to just anyone."

She glared at him. "So I am not just anyone? Finally?"

He paused. "You haven't been just anyone for a long time," he said.

"Then why are you only telling me now?" she said, a little red in the face.

"You didn't ask," he said. "Since those first days, you never asked."

Miss Maggie made a sound like Mouse did when we pulled ticks off her neck. "Is that what I should call you then?"

Osh shook his head. "That's what I used to be. I'm Osh now. And Daniel."

I thought Miss Maggie might blow apart like a dandelion head in the wind. "But you just said your name was important to you! You just scolded me for calling you Daniel!"

"It is important to me, but it's part of what I used to be. You're part of what I am now, so Daniel will do."

At which Miss Maggie turned as pink and fluttery as a primrose.

"Why don't you come sit in the shade while I catch us some lunch," Osh said.

At which Miss Maggie took a long breath. She smoothed her hair away from her face and put her hands on her cheeks. "Shade sounds good," she said.

"And will you both come back to Penikese with me?" I asked, eager to get that resolved while we were still in the business of sorting things out.

Osh sighed. "You're like a dog with a bone," he said.

"Of course we will," Miss Maggie said. "You're not going anywhere alone this time. We're going to put this straight, once and for all."

In the end, even Osh agreed to that. He seemed calmer, not so sad, now that he'd said some things he'd been holding back. Some of them for a long time.

Chapter 27

*I*t rained the next day. And the one after that. A windy rain that stirred up the sea and kept us on the island.

"Penikese will still be there when we get to it," Osh said. He always had plenty to do, rain or shine, and didn't mind a chance to make paints and mend his gear.

But I was eager for another crossing, mostly to tend the graves where my parents were buried. And to find what they'd left for me.

I thought I knew where it was, but the rain gave me time to think, so that's what I did. Until a midday knock startled both of us to our feet.

It was not a Miss Maggie knock.

She was with them, though. The two police officers from the mainland. Officers Kelly and Reardon.

All three wore oilskin ponchos, which they shed and shook

out, one by one, before coming into the house. Miss Maggie had come barefoot and her hair was down around her face, both of which were unusual for her, and I wondered at the change.

The officers wore muck boots, but their trousers were nonetheless dark with seawater. As they stood looking around at our unusual home, puddles formed at their feet.

Osh said to Miss Maggie, "So you sent your message."

"Indeed, I did," she said. "Did you imagine that I wouldn't?"

She turned to the policemen. "This," she said, her hand on Osh's shoulder, "is the artist who drew the likeness of the man we saw on Penikese. The same man Crow saw in New Bedford."

Officer Kelly flipped open his little notebook and licked the tip of his pencil. "Your name?" he said.

Osh glared at Miss Maggie. "Daniel," he said through his teeth, looking away from the policemen.

"Daniel what?"

He paused. "Fisher," he said.

I was glad the officers weren't looking at me. Miss Maggie's eyes, too, grew round for a moment when he said that.

They turned to me, and Osh sat again among his painting things, facing his easel. "You saw the man again?" Officer Kelly asked me. "In New Bedford?"

"I did," I said. "And I know his name, too."

That brought them up short, though Officer Reardon smiled as if I'd said something funny. "And are you a young Sherlock Holmes?" he said, bending a little, his hands on his knees.

I leaned closer and said, "His name is James Kendall. From Carville, Louisiana. Or near there."

Officer Reardon straightened up. "And how do you know that?"

I explained about the letter from Nurse Evelyn. "She used to work on Penikese when it was a leper colony, and I was curious about some of the patients there, so I wrote to her. And she wrote back and told me some things about that man."

Officer Reardon made a face. "Why would she do that?"

I sighed, worried now that the story was coming out like this, so tangled up that I thought I might trip on it. "Because I asked her some questions about a patient who dug up a necklace on Penikese and gave it to her. And she told Mr. Kendall about that. And he stole it and disappeared. And then we saw a big man on Penikese, with a southern accent, who had dug holes all over the island."

Officer Kelly was writing in his notebook. Officer Reardon squinted at me, frowning.

"That's quite a story," he said.

"And a hard one to follow," said Officer Kelly. "Where is this letter of yours?"

I hadn't thought they'd want it. "It's my letter," I said.

"Yes, but it's evidence," he replied, an edge to his voice, "and I'd like to take it with me."

I looked at Miss Maggie. She nodded. "If you want to catch him," she said.

I looked to Osh for his advice, but he was intent on his work, his back to us.

I went to the cinnamon box and fetched the letter. Before I gave it to the officers, I took it out of the envelope and kept back the last page, where Nurse Evelyn had answered my words with her own.

"Here, here," Officer Reardon said, reaching out his hand. "What's that about?"

"It's private," I said. "Nothing to do with Mr. Kendall." I handed him the first page of the letter. "This is the part about him."

They both read it silently, looking up at me from time to time.

When they were done, Officer Kelly tucked it back in the envelope and then inside his notebook. "Well, this should make things somewhat easier," he said. "Now tell us what happened in New Bedford."

I told them the parts that mattered to them, about Mr. Kendall appearing near the dock and then visiting the pawnbroker. "I think he sold a gold locket in there," I said. "But I don't know why he looked so angry when he came out."

Officer Reardon chuckled. "He likely got a lot less than he wanted for it," he said.

"Do you think he stole that necklace, too?"

They both nodded. "He sounds like a proper thief to me," Officer Kelly said. "But not a very smart one to stay so close by."

Officer Kelly put away his notebook. "You three be careful now," he said. "I don't expect he's stupid enough to come back to the islands, but I've seen plenty of stranger and stupider things in my time."

Officer Reardon nodded. "You'd be amazed what people will do when money's involved," he said. "We'll see what we can do about this Mr. Kendall, though I doubt he goes by that name here." He turned to Osh. "The picture will help."

Osh nodded. "Good," he said, and did not show his face again until they were gone.

When the officers had left, I imagined them returning to the mainland, writing up a report, telling stories in the pub, spreading the news that the mysterious southerner really had been digging for treasure.

"Do you think people will come out here now," I asked Miss Maggie, "looking for whatever Mr. Kendall didn't find?"

Osh put down his brush and rubbed the back of his neck. "How do you know he didn't find it?" he asked.

Which gave me a start. I was stunned that this possibility hadn't occurred to me.

"Well, I guess I don't," I said slowly. "I guess I thought he gave up and took off after we saw him out there."

"Maybe so," Osh said. "Maybe not."

"Which will do nothing to stop a thousand fools from

digging up the rest of the island once they hear what he was after," Miss Maggie said.

"You don't think he really found anything, do you?" I hated the thought that whatever Susanna had kept safe for me was in a pawnshop somewhere.

"No," Osh said. "I don't think he did."

"Nor do I," Miss Maggie said briskly. "But somebody else might be luckier than he was. So we'll go out there as soon as the weather clears."

The others came before the rain stopped.

Miss Maggie heard about it at the grocery and came straightaway to tell us.

I was sitting at the kitchen table, doing my sums—which was usually what I did on the second day of a long rain—when she arrived, bringing a good deal of wind and wet in with her.

"One day," she said. "It took just one day for the first of them to come." She took off her poncho and hung it by the door. Again, she was barefoot, her feet little and white. "Those police officers must have stood at the top of Nobska Light with a megaphone and shouted about it."

Osh didn't seem concerned. "Crow knows where it is. They don't."

I put down my pencil. "I do?"

"Don't you?" he said.

I thought about the feather on my cheek and the one on the wall of the leper cottage.

I thought about the two lambs on Penikese.

About everything Nurse Evelyn had written. And everything she hadn't.

"Yes," I said. "I think I do know where it is. And you do, too, don't you?"

Osh nodded. "Only one place it could be."

"Well?" Miss Maggie said. "Are you going to tell me?"

"Of course," I said.

And we did.

When we were done, Miss Maggie looked sad.

"We'll wait for them to leave, then," she said. "And when they're gone, and we have Penikese to ourselves, we'll go out there again and finish what Susanna started."

Chapter 28

*A*fter another day, the rain stopped, but the parade of treasure hunters from the mainland did not. Some of the islanders went over, too, to muck around. When they sailed back to Cuttyhunk, they spoke of whole families over to Penikese from Woods Hole and beyond, the children with their little tin spades, even the mothers in their dresses and bonnets digging a hole or two before laying out picnics on the Penikese bluffs, everyone playing games along the moors afterward before heading home.

But there were also a few rough, no-nonsense men with proper gear and hard hands who went about their work with no silliness of any kind.

These were the men I feared—the ones who dug and dug and dug—single-minded and deliberate. If anyone found Susanna's treasure, it would be one of these unsmiling men.

I wondered if Mr. Kendall had come back over from New Bedford to dig some more, camouflaged by the crowd of others like him. I wondered if he was out there right now, tearing up that land.

I listened to all the talk of Penikese—outside the grocery, in the post office yard—and counted the hours until all those strangers tired of the hunt and went away. I wanted fiercely for them to go, but not because of the treasure. These were the same clean people who would never have stepped foot on Penikese otherwise. Certainly not to bring soup to the lepers there. Or blankets. Or prayers when they died. And I waited, impatiently, for them to be gone.

While I waited, I watched for the *Shearwater* to sail through our waters again.

It was too early for her to be back from Portland yet, even if she had not gone on to some other, more distant port. But I watched anyway, my thoughts never far from the sailor who looked like me.

I spent the mornings at my chores, one eye on the sea, and then, from the top of a drumlin, spent some time looking north, my old spyglass ready.

I even climbed up Lookout Hill to ask the surfman there if he'd keep an eye out, his long glass far superior to mine, his single job to watch for ships coming through.

"I'm but one lookout," he said, not unkindly, "and I've but

one purpose here. But I'll try to keep it in mind, and I'll mention it to the others, but no promises, Crow. Unless she's in trouble, I'm likely to miss her. Best if you keep watch yourself."

So I did, when I could.

And I made up my mind that when I did see that old schooner with a long green pennant flying from its mainmast, I would be on the next boat to New Bedford, this time in our own skiff if need be. This time with Osh and Miss Maggie, to meet the schooner when she moored.

I saw other ships sail through, some of them flying the striped pennant that told pilots to come help them navigate the Graveyard, past Sow and Pigs Reef, and into the deeper safety of Buzzards Bay. But none of them flew a long green pennant.

The *Shearwater* was a smallish ship whose captain surely knew these waters well enough to manage on his own. Which meant he might slip past me and across to New Bedford without giving me a chance to chase her into port.

"No point looking for her so late in the day," Osh said as we stood on our little beach one evening, Mouse with us in the long twilight, the sky fading to gray, the empty sea surging past. "If she appears now, we can't follow. I won't sail out as night comes, even if there were a way to catch her before she moored."

He, too, looked out toward Sow and Pigs, but he was not looking for anything. I knew that, for him, the rising moon was all.

Mouse paid no attention to anything except a mole crab that

decided it had lived long enough and tunneled up through the sand directly between her front paws.

"But if I see her, at least I'll know she's come back to New Bedford," I said.

"Which wouldn't help you find your brother," he said. "Have you ever seen sailors when they reach port?"

I shook my head.

"They furl their sails at double-time, then off they go," he said, "into the city like mice into grain."

"I'd still find him," I said. Though I remembered how, even in daylight, the city had seemed too big. Too confusing.

"I believe you could," Osh said, "if anyone could." And he let me do my waiting and watching without much interference. And he didn't try again to distract me as the days went by, no old schooner among them.

On the morning of the ninth day since I'd first seen the *Shearwater*, the rain came back, and I woke up knowing that Penikese had waited long enough.

For once, I was up before Osh, though he was stirring in his bed as I slipped past him.

The stove was cold, so I twisted a length of grocery paper into a wick and coiled it in the firebox. We kept a bin of driftwood twigs nearby, perfect kindling that caught easily when I lit the paper and blew gently on the flame. More driftwood on top, and

I soon had a good fire going. By the time Osh joined me, yawning and stretching, I had his coffee at the simmer.

"Did I do something good?" he asked me, knuckling his eyes like a child.

"I don't know," I said. "Did you?"

He shrugged. "Then did *you* do something bad?"

"Like what?"

He shrugged again. "In all our years, you've never made me coffee," he said.

"Well, since you're going over to Penikese with me today, it's the least I can do."

Osh filled his mug with coffee and opened the door for Mouse. She stepped out into the rain, back, out again, and then arranged herself on the threshold, just at the edge of dry ground.

Osh leaned over her and took a good look at the sky. "In this rain?"

I remembered what Miss Maggie had once said to me. "We're not made of sugar," I told him. "We won't melt."

Osh frowned. "You sound like Miss Maggie."

"We'll probably be the only ones over there on a day like this," I said. "Especially since no one's dug up anything yet but rabbit bones and an old ax head."

Osh drank his coffee. "I meant to go after some bass today," he said.

"They'll still be there tomorrow," I replied, cracking two eggs into a skillet.

He gave me a hard look. "If you think imitating Miss Maggie is going to convince me, you're wrong."

"Go sit down," I said, tending the eggs. "Your breakfast is almost ready."

"I'm warning you," he said. But he sat at the table, both hands wrapped around his mug. "Last thing I need is two Miss Maggies," he muttered.

But no matter what he said, we both knew that Osh would be in trouble without the one he had.

Chapter 29

The rain was nothing but a heavy mist by the time we set sail, armed with a shovel and canvas bags to carry back whatever we might find, even if it was only woadwaxen.

Miss Maggie was in trousers for our unusual quest, her hair stuffed into an old newsy cap, her little hands in work gloves. She dressed like that often when she went after her sheep or helped one of her cows with a calving—all business and matter-of-fact—but the pink in her cheeks made me think of roses.

"You look pretty," I said to her as we sailed out through the Narrows.

"Oh, go on," she said.

But I could tell she was pleased. She glanced at Osh.

"Coming about," he said, and we ducked our heads and shifted to the starboard bench as the boom swung across and we tacked past the last of the land.

It began to rain again in earnest as we crossed to Penikese. Miss Maggie and I raised our hoods and bowed our heads while Osh carried on as if he were a seal, unfazed by a little wet.

A catboat was just leaving the harbor as we sailed in. A single sailor, slumped in the stern, tipped his cap wearily as we sailed past. "Good luck," he yelled. "Been diggin' for three days. Nothing on that island but birds and birds."

We waved back, glad to see no other craft in the harbor. Gladder, still, when the rain tapered off again the minute we pulled up on the beach and tied the skiff to a post.

We already knew where we were going, so I didn't need to say a word as we collected the shovel and sacks and began, single file, across the island.

I led the way.

There were holes everywhere, and of course the mounds of dirt dug up alongside them. Crossing the moor in the dark would be a risky business, but we were able to navigate our way just fine and in no time came up along the opposite shore.

The graveyard was as we'd left it.

It hurt me to know that children had frolicked on this island just days ago. Here, in this place where "monsters" had once lived.

But the fear that had for years kept the treasure hunters away from Penikese persisted enough to keep them away from the graveyard where the lepers were buried, my parents among them, and I was grateful for that fear. It had kept this small plot of land safe.

As I stood at the gate, Osh and Miss Maggie at my back, I pictured Susanna in her bed, Elvan at her side, both of them watching as Nurse Evelyn wrapped me tenderly in the softest cloth they had. I pictured them wanting to kiss me good-bye, careful with their tears, holding each other because they could not hold me. I pictured their agony as I drifted away on the tide. Heard their prayers. Heard the answer. I pictured Elvan with the treasure that Susanna had found. Tucking it into a small trunk. Nurse Evelyn helping him carry it across the moon-blackened moors. Burying it in the graveyard, his poor hands terrible, his body aching with such work. Carving MORGAN into the wood that marked the new "grave." And then returning to Susanna just as I reached a fresh shore. Just as Osh woke, perhaps at the cry of a crow nearby.

The gate was latched, the ground inside the fence undisturbed.

We stopped first at the graves where my parents were buried. Miss Maggie touched the top of each marker.

Osh said something in his other language.

I didn't have any words. The ground where I stood seemed warmer than the moors. The wind here more musical. How could I miss the people buried here? Parents I had never known?

But I did.

Then we stood around the grave with the wooden marker that read MORGAN, and Osh said, "Are you sure about this?"

I nodded. "My mother wanted everyone to think I'd died," I said. "She didn't want anyone coming to look for me or treating me like a leper, whether I was one or not."

"Which they do anyway," he said.

Miss Maggie touched his arm. "Hush about all that," she said.

"I want to do this myself," I said, a quiver of fear in my voice. Whether it was a real grave or not, this was a piece of holy ground close by the remains of my mother and father. I hated the thought of digging here.

But before I had a chance to do another thing, we heard a shout from across the moor and looked to see two men coming over a rise toward us, waving as they walked.

"Who are they?" I asked, squinting into the distance.

"Nobody we want here," Osh said.

I laid the shovel flat in the tall grass and we left the grave-yard, shutting the gate behind us, walking quickly toward the two men.

Officers Reardon and Kelly.

"What can they want here?" Miss Maggie said.

"They can't have come for us," Osh said, pulling his hood closer around his face. "Nobody knows we're here."

He was right. When we met them, midway across the open ground, the officers were as surprised to see us as we were to see them. "We never expected to find you three," Officer Kelly said.

"And we never expected you two, either," Miss Maggie said.

"We've come to look for the man you drew," Officer Reardon said, nodding at Osh. "Mr. Kendall."

Miss Maggie took a half step closer to Osh, who bowed his head a little, the gathered mist running off his hood in a stream.

"We took that picture of him to New Bedford, to the pawn-broker and all along the waterfront. And this morning someone came and told us they'd seen him just yesterday, heading out in a skiff, most likely the one he stole from the gamekeeper. We figure he heard we were asking about him. Maybe he's finally running. So the precincts all along the coast are watching for him, but we're covering our own ground."

"And all the other Elizabeths, too?" I asked. There were islands in the chain that had little more than sheep living on them. No better place for someone laying low.

They were, they said, as best they could. "Lots of people looking now," Officer Reardon said. "If he's still around here, someone will see him."

"But I still don't understand why he'd stay where he's most likely to get caught," Miss Maggie said.

"Nor do we," Officer Kelly said. "It makes no sense."

"Unless he's still after whatever's buried here," Officer Reardon said.

We all looked around at the pocked moor, the hundreds of dirt hills, the mist hanging like still smoke above the ravaged ground.

"Less likely to find it now than before when he was the only one looking," Officer Kelly said. "But we're making sure. We'll have a look in the buildings and then be off." But as they turned toward the big hospital and the littler cottages, he paused and asked, "When we saw your skiff, we thought maybe it was his. Why are you three here, yourselves?"

I looked to Osh, but he was busy looking at the sea, his back to the rest of us. After a moment, Miss Maggie said, "To harvest plants for his paints," she said. "And to visit the graveyard. We come out here from time to time, now that there's no one else to tend it."

They seemed satisfied with that answer, though Officer Reardon kept his eyes on her for a beat too long. "That's mighty nice of you," he said thoughtfully.

At which she stood up a little straighter and lifted her chin. "Just plain decent is what it is," she said.

And we headed off toward the graveyard, the officers toward the hospital, the rain starting up again.

The swales and small hills soon hid the officers from us, and us from them, but I felt very anxious about digging up a grave when they were on the island.

"Anyone could come at any time," Miss Maggie said as we stood in the rain around the little grave. "Including that Mr. Kendall."

"Dig," Osh said. "Or let's go." He kept glancing in the direction of the hospital, then out across Buzzards Bay as if Mr. Sloan's stolen skiff might appear at any moment, that bully man in the stern.

So I dug.

It was easier after the first cut, but I went carefully, my shovel slicing through the sandy soil, for fear I would hit something too hard. Surely not a casket. Surely nothing of the kind. There was no baby buried here. I knew that. But I still went carefully, and my heart clenched when I hit something.

With Osh standing watch and Miss Maggie at my back, whispering to herself, I knelt down and went on digging with my hands, scooping the dirt aside, until I had cleared the top of a metal trunk as long as the distance from my elbow to the tips of my fingers. My shovel had dented the top of it, but it was still whole and sound even after years in the earth.

I cleared the sides enough to see a handle at either end. "Come help me, Osh," I said.

He did, taking one handle as I took the other, and we tried to lift it free of the grave. But the wet hole had a good grip on the box, and it took help from Miss Maggie, too, before we managed to drag it up out of the hole and onto level ground.

It was far too heavy to hold nothing but bones.

We backed away from it.

The lid was closed with a hasp and pin, but no lock.

"Open it," Osh said, looking over his shoulder.

Miss Maggie, her hands over her eyes, took a step away as I knelt again next to the little trunk.

I pulled out the pin and let it drop to the length of its chain.

"I'm afraid," I said, though I was sure of what was inside.

"Then put it back and let's go," Osh said. He sounded afraid himself.

"Open it, Crow," Miss Maggie said. "This is why we came. This is what Susanna wanted."

The lid stuck enough so I had to work it open. When it suddenly fell back on its hinges, I too fell back and sat on the wet ground, speechless.

Inside was the sort of treasure I had never expected to see. Gold in coins and ingots. Beautiful, beautiful, beautiful jewelry. The kind that queens wear. The kind that Captain Kidd had buried on islands like Penikese.

The rain made the treasure more beautiful still. I could only imagine what it might look like in the sun.

"I thought there would be a little sack buried here," I whispered. *"With a bracelet or another ring. Or maybe some coin."*

Osh stood above me and stared, his face a picture of shock and worry.

"We have to get this out of here as fast as we can," he said. "This will mean terrible things if people know about it."

"Susanna," Miss Maggie whispered. "Your mother was re-markable, Crow. To bury this for you when she might have spent it to buy whatever ease she could."

"If the state let her spend it on this place," Osh said. "Which is doubtful." He knelt next to me and began to fill the canvas bags. Spread between them, the treasure was manageable. Osh hung one sack from each shoulder.

"Close the trunk," he said, "and bury it again, Crow." He started back for the skiff. "And bring the shovel. Hurry now."

I pictured the officers heading back for their own boat and crossing paths with us as they came.

I did what he said, as fast as I could, sorry to leave the grave looking new, a clue for anyone coming along after us.

At the last moment, I dropped the shovel and hurried to the graves where Susanna and Elvan were buried.

I put my open hand on the marker at Elvan's grave. He was a stranger, my father. A man long dead and gone. But I said some things to him and hoped he would know me a little that way.

At my mother's grave, I knelt and leaned my forehead against the wet ground, my eyes open, as close to her bones as I could get.

And then I gathered up the shovel and ran.

Chapter 30

We reached the shore and loaded the bags and the shovel into the skiff just moments before the officers came over the bluff and headed for their own boat, tied up at the dock.

The tide had gone out some, and I helped Osh push the beached skiff afloat. Then Osh and Miss Maggie climbed in while I stood in the shallows, hanging on to the bow.

The policemen waved to us from the dock, we waved back, and I jumped into the skiff, giving it a good shove into deeper water so Osh could lower the centerboard while I hoisted the sail. Miss Maggie, in the stern, looked smaller than she ever had.

It was a quiet crossing, none of us in the mood for talk. I was pretty sure that most people would have been whooping with joy over a find such as ours, but we were not.

None of us cared about money, as long as we had food and fuel and boots in the winter.

None of us wanted to bring the world down around our ears. None of us wanted anything further to do with Mr. Kendall, who would be furious if he learned that we had found what he had failed to find.

Miss Maggie and Osh had both been in the wider world and found it lacking. Though I had never strayed beyond the nearest city, even I had seen enough to know that I wasn't ready yet for what was waiting.

"We have to keep this a secret," I said.

Osh nodded. "Unless we have to, we won't tell a soul," he said.

We listened for a while to the rain having its own conversation with the sea, the wind chiming in when it had something to say.

"And we can't hide it on our island," Osh finally said, and it was clear that he'd been thinking about what to do with Susanna's treasure.

"Why not?" I asked. True, our island wasn't very big, but I couldn't imagine hiding it anywhere else.

"Bad enough that the police have been there. I don't want anyone else looking too hard at where we live."

"Why not?" I asked.

Osh didn't answer at first. Miss Maggie and I waited patiently.

"Before I came to the islands, I had to give up some things." He paused, his face dark in the shadow of his hood. He gave the tiller a hard push away from him and then pulled it back. "Coming about," he said, and Miss Maggie and I ducked under the boom and resettled to port.

"What things?" I asked.

He shook his head. "It doesn't matter. I'm not interested in all that anymore. But if someone tries to force us off the island, I'll fight to stay. And I don't want to if I don't have to."

"Why would they do that?" I asked.

Miss Maggie, her eyes on Osh, said, "Because that's what people do when they think something doesn't belong to you. Like taking the treasure because it was buried on state land, even if it belonged to someone else before that. And like claiming a little island that nobody else would ever have thought of wanting, until someone else wanted it."

I thought about such things for the rest of the crossing, looking at the Elizabeths as if I'd never seen them before.

"But what makes it ours?" I asked, though I didn't want to. The island was my home, and I, too, would fight to stay there if I had to.

Osh smiled, which confused me even more. "We may call it that, but it isn't," he said. "It's nobody's."

When we came ashore, wet and weary, Mouse scampered down from the rocks to tell us how to furl the sail, and she fairly danced with curiosity as we lugged the bags of treasure up to the cottage.

After we'd put on clean clothes and locked the door, Osh and I spread the treasure out in front of the hearth while Miss Maggie lit a fire in the stove.

"You two must live on air," she said. She was wearing a pair of trousers and an old shirt that Osh had given her until her clothes dried out. She looked ridiculous, everything rolled up and tucked in. "There's nothing here worth cooking."

"I'll pick some mussels," I said, scrambling to my feet.

But Osh shook his head. "Tide's high."

"Well, we don't need to cook," I told her. "We have bread and cheese. And the last of the strawberries you brought yesterday."

Which was a fine dinner, and afterward we lit a fire though it was warm and sat before it, sipping hot tea, while Miss Maggie's clothes dried. The treasure, spread out between us on the floor, looked like a bright garden.

Mouse chose a long silver chain as big around as my finger to drag into a corner and wrestle into submission.

"Give that back," I said, trading the chain for a bit of string.

"Which is your favorite?" I asked Miss Maggie.

She set down her mug and bent closer to consider her choices. "They're all too fancy for me," she said, leaning back. "What would the sheep think if I went out to the moor in diamonds?"

But Osh reached down and plucked a single strand of pearls from the tangle.

Miss Maggie closed her eyes as he slipped it over her head.

When he returned to his chair, she looked at him and ran her fingers over the pearls.

"Thank you, but plain is fine with me," she said.

"And with me," Osh replied.

"And me," I said. "But they're much prettier *on* you than not."

"And they're much plainer than diamonds," Osh said.

She closed her eyes again and sighed. "What an extraordinary day."

"Tomorrow we hide all this," Osh said. "And then things can get back to the way they were."

———

When her clothes were dry, Miss Maggie put them on again and slipped into her poncho. She made sure the pearls were tucked away out of sight before she left.

"Life is going to seem very straightforward after all this adventure," she mused.

"And now some quiet," Osh said. "And work to do."

She rolled her eyes. "And work to do," she echoed. "Of course."

When he pulled on his own poncho and began to follow her out the door, she said, "I can make my own way, thank you."

But he paid her no attention, and I stood in the doorway and watched as he settled her in the skiff and rowed her across the channel. On the far side, he helped her onto the sand. They said a few words to each other. And then he turned and rowed the skiff back home, tucking it up above the wrack line, and coming back inside.

For quite some time, we sat by the fire and looked at the treasure some more. It gleamed and sparkled in the firelight.

"I hope this won't change you," Osh said.

"Why would it change me?"

He chose his words. "I've seen it happen," he said. "People don't want much until they have plenty, and then they want more and more."

I was sure having the treasure wouldn't change me that way, and I said as much. "When I think about what to do with all this, I think about giving it away. How lovely that would be."

Osh looked at me so hard I thought I might break. "What's wrong?" I asked him.

"Not a thing," he said. "I'm just looking at you. Exactly as you are right now. And not because you'll change, though you will, of course. Treasure or not. But because if I could have built a human being, I would have built you. Just so."

Nobody had ever said anything that good about me.

We watched the fire for a while. Mouse decided that I needed something in my lap and jumped up to nuzzle my face.

The fire rearranged itself, sparks flying, and the rain began again, hard enough to make itself heard on the rooftop.

If I never lived another day in my life, I would be fine with that, I decided.

Or I would be after the schooner *Shearwater* came home and I'd shared with my brother the treasure that our mother, and then I, had found.

Chapter 31

I woke in the night and lay still, trying to understand what had brought me up out of a dream in which I stood at the very end of a dock, a schooner under full sail sweeping past, almost close enough to touch, my brother at the rail, reaching.

Osh was snoring softly nearby. Mouse was curled up at the foot of my bed, as usual. The rain had stopped, and there wasn't enough wind to wake me. The fire had gone out, and day had not yet broken.

I decided that nothing was amiss, but the very idea of the treasure still in the house made me jittery. Perhaps it had woken me up.

Before going to sleep, we had put the treasure back in the canvas bags and slipped it under my bed, out of sight.

I thought about where to hide it.

One by one, I considered and rejected every spot except two.

I considered them from every angle, pictured the treasure safe in them, and made my decision as morning came slowly on.

But other things were not as clear. Other things did not make as much sense.

How was it possible to think, with just one mind, about a woman, her hands twisted, her body as rough and worn as the moors of Penikese itself—poor and tough and shrinking toward a terrible end, toward a cold grave on a bluff with not one tree for shade, no simple bench where a mourner might sit for a while to watch the sea and wish for something better?

How was it possible to think, with that same mind, about perfect, immortal diamonds forged in the hot belly of the earth—indestructible, endless, capable of binding all color into one clear and icy light, nothing lost?

How was it possible that they had been buried side by side for years while so many people dreamed of finding one of them, while just I—one, single girl and no one else in the entire world—longed for the other.

And now I had found them both.

And now for me they would always be one and the same.

As quietly as I could, I got up and fetched an old coffee tin where Osh sometimes kept seeds he collected once the garden was spent. Then I carefully tugged the bags of treasure out from under my bed.

In the almost darkness, I couldn't see much, but I could feel the cold smoothness of the gold ingots, the pictures pressed into the coins, the perfect facets of the gemstones.

I combed carefully through both bags, stopping often to hold a piece up close to my face, glad when the growing light let me see some color, and chose a few: all of them small enough to fit in the coffee tin, all of them nearly ordinary compared to the others, but also, in my eyes, the most beautiful. Among them, a necklace with a single sapphire pendant. A cuff bracelet set with ruby flowers. A gold ring so delicate, so simple, that it must have been worn by a good woman.

I thought about her. About the other people who had once owned these treasures before they'd lost them. If I'd known how to give it all back, I would have. But it had found its complicated way to me, and I would cherish the treasure while I had it. I would cherish it because it had come from my mother and because it would always belong to both of us, even after it found its complicated way to someone else. Even though I was simply a stop on its travels, just as the island was but one stop on mine.

The thought made me feel fragile.

And it made me understand better what Osh saw when he looked at me.

When Osh showed signs of waking and the shorebirds began to announce the day, I tucked the special things I'd chosen into the tin, closed it up tight, and thought about where to hide this smaller, better treasure.

Which was when I remembered what Osh always said: If you want to hide something, leave it in plain sight.

So I tiptoed back to where I'd found the tin and put it on the shelf again.

Osh wouldn't need it until the garden was spent and he was ready to harvest its seed. And I would have told him about this keepsake long before that. Explained why it was important. Really, as soon as I could explain that to myself.

I hadn't put aside this small portion of treasure to sell, though we could if we had to. Not to wear—like Miss Maggie, I was happy enough with plain. Just to hold in my hands, and look at, while I tried to know what I knew in my bones, to remember the faces I'd seen for only moments, when my eyes were still foggy with birth. The voices I'd heard just once, before I'd been sent away.

I waited until Osh had his coffee before I told him where I'd decided to hide the sacks of treasure.

He listened carefully, his head tipped to one side. "Two places?" he said.

"So if somebody finds one of them, we'll still have the other." I cut two slices of hard bread and spread some apple butter on top of them.

He nodded. "You're a smart Crow." Osh sipped his coffee thoughtfully. "But perhaps we should give the whole thing away right off, as you said. To a hospital. Or an orphanage. Or a school."

I took the bread to the table and sat down. "The whole

thing?" I myself had said that it would be lovely to give it away, but I hadn't thought I'd be asked to do that. I'd thought it would be up to me. Which it was, I supposed. "Half of it is for Jason," I said.

Osh shrugged. "That's fair," he said.

"But maybe I will give away my half," I said. I watched Mouse at her bath, licking the back of her paw and then dragging it over one ear, again and again. "Can I think about it?"

"You can do whatever you want," he said.

"Then I will," I said. "I'll think about it. But can we hide it until I figure things out?"

He finished his coffee and got up for more. "We can," he said. "If that's what you want."

We did just that, later the same day.

First, we divided the treasure into two piles, one bigger and heavier than the other. We then rolled each pile into the middle of a piece of oilcloth, tucked the ends of the cloth over, and tied the bundle with plenty of wire twisted with fishing line. We put each bundle into a canvas sack, then into a second one for good measure, and tied up the neck with more fishing line. To the smaller of the two bundles, we tied a length of rope.

"That should do the trick," Osh said when we were through.

The first, bigger bundle was easier to hide since we could do that during our regular chores. No one, seeing us, would think twice about it.

The second one would be more challenging, I realized, but not too difficult.

"I'll take care of the rest," I said when Osh and I returned to the house for lunch.

"Just be careful," he said. "Will you tell Miss Maggie about it?"

I nodded. "Sure. If she's there. And later on, if she's not."

"And about the first one?"

"Of course," I said. "Wouldn't you?"

He hesitated for only a moment. "Yes. She's in this as much as we are. But she likes her life as it is." He grew serious. "Think about her when you do things, Crow. Think about what they'll mean."

"I will," I said. "Nothing bad is going to happen, Osh."

But he had nothing to say to that. He gave me my lunch and ate his own, both of us busy with our thoughts, and didn't say anything more about the treasure until I was ready to hide the second bundle on Cuttyhunk.

Then Osh said, "Anybody ever tries to take that from you, you let go of it. Understand?"

I thought about what he'd said on the skiff coming home from Penikese. About fighting for the island if he had to. I reminded him of that.

"I can't hand someone an island, wrapped in a piece of oilcloth. And I can't take it with me, either." He sighed. "I won't fight to keep the island, Crow. It doesn't belong to me. But I'll fight to stay on it. This," he said, nodding at the bundle, "you can hand over quite easily."

I thought he might be right, especially since I'd already hidden keepsakes in the coffee tin. But, "Nothing bad will happen," I repeated.

And then I went off toward Cuttyhunk, prepared, if I saw anyone, to say that I was taking quahogs to Miss Maggie for her supper.

Luckily, I didn't see a soul along the way, and when I got to Miss Maggie's I found both the house and the barn empty, so I was able to hide the bundle properly without anyone the wiser, though I had a few scrapes to show for it.

I felt much better as I walked back along the path toward the bass stands. Tidy. A burden gone.

As I walked, I repeated what I'd said to Osh—"Nothing bad will happen"—and I believed it. But believing something doesn't always make it so.

Chapter 32

Nothing much—good or bad—happened for a while after that. When I told Miss Maggie that I had hidden part of the treasure at her place, she held up a hand and said, "Don't tell me where. If I need to know, I'll ask you."

"And I'll tell you," I said. "Just let me know if you come across it, and I'll find a better hiding place."

"I will," she agreed.

And we left it at that.

For those few long summer days, I was able to focus on what was in front of me, working alongside Osh and Miss Maggie and catching up on my lessons and reading new books Miss Maggie had borrowed from the library. But I also spent time watching the Graveyard for ships coming through.

I knew that the *Shearwater* had probably passed by while I was busy with other things, but I was sure that I could count on

Mrs. Pelham at the hospital in New Bedford to tell Jason how to find me when he went to see her again.

I expected that one day he might knock on our door, out of the blue. And that would be fine. But I confess that I was impatient. I didn't want to wait that long.

So up to a hilltop I trudged each day, and the heavy heat of summer made me glad for the bigger winds I found there.

I still saw people sailing to and from Penikese from time to time, and I imagined them digging up what was left of the moors.

I guessed that no one would go into the leper graveyard. Of all the places where a treasure might be buried, the graveyard was the least likely, most of it already devoted to the bones of the Penikese lepers. And those old bones were another reason for people to dig elsewhere, despite how foolish it was to be afraid of something so long dead and buried. But I had learned that fear was fear, most of it not very smart, and I was happy if it gave the little grave time to heal.

I wondered what someone would think if they found the ground there disturbed. Nearly everyone believed that a baby was resting in that ground. A leper baby. And who would want to meddle with such a grave?

But that was the problem. Anyone digging in such a place must have had good reason to think that the treasure was buried there.

And the policemen had seen us at the graveyard, in the rain.

The thief, Mr. Kendall, knew that we'd been out there, too. And I'd asked him if he knew anything about a baby.

If he ever went back to Penikese and saw that little grave all turned up and raw, he would know. I was sure he would.

I shook my head clean of such thoughts.

What was done was done.

The treasure was hidden well.

I knew where I'd come from, finally, and that I had a brother somewhere.

I still had what I'd always had, and more, and no one hurt in the process.

But as I sat in the evening wind and scanned the ocean going slowly gray, I wondered why I felt so sad.

When night came, it did not fall, as people say it does. Beyond the bright crown of the earth, the heavens were always dark. Here, on this lonely hill, tinier than the smallest suggestion of a moment, I watched the darkness rise up from the ground to meet the steady darkness overhead, as if the two worlds had been waiting for the sun to go so they could touch again.

And I, too, was dark. Invisible. Silent.

Across the bay, New Bedford squatted like a toad. Such a dirty, noisy, greedy place. But over there, I'd been Crow, just Crow, a stranger among strangers. Nothing more. Nothing less.

Here, in this clean and beautiful place, among people I had always known, I wasn't sure where I fit. And that, I decided, was the sad part.

There were a few islanders on the porch of the grocery, trading gossip in the shade, when I came up the path the next morning, a dime in my pocket.

"Good morning, Crow," said Mr. Benson, the pilot who spent much of his time at the grocery between jobs.

The others turned to watch me climb the steps to the porch. Mrs. Aaronson, who baked pies for the inn, opened the screen door so I could go inside.

People always opened doors for me whenever they could. Looking on, a stranger might think they were just being nice. But I knew otherwise: The islanders preferred that I keep my hands to myself.

Everyone stopped talking as I stood there at the open door.

I walked over to where Mr. Benson sat in one of the porch chairs, smoking his pipe.

"Good morning to you, too, Mr. Benson," I said. I held out my hand, as I'd seen people so often do.

He looked at me. Looked around at the other islanders. Looked back at me.

And slowly took my hand. Shook it twice. Let it go.

I watched for him to wipe it on his pant leg or grip the hot bowl of his pipe, but he didn't. He simply laid it in his lap and looked me steadily in the eye until, after a moment, I was the one to look away.

"If you're not going in, Crow, the sandflies are," Mrs. Aaronson said.

So I went into the grocery.

She shut the door gently.

And I heard the conversation on the porch start up again. They talked about what storms we might expect that summer. A liniment that eased bruises. A trip off-island. News from Boston. Nothing about me.

Mr. Higgins, the grocer, came out from behind the counter. "Can I get something for you, Crow?"

I thought about how eager he always was to help me when I came to fetch something for Miss Maggie or Osh. He always rushed to ask me what I wanted, picked it out himself, put it in a bag, and handed it over.

In the past, I'd always peered into the case of chocolates and pointed out my choices so he could pluck them from their little paper nests and wrap them up for me.

Instead, today, I went straight to the big jar of jelly beans on the counter by the till, took off the top, reached inside for the scoop, and measured out my own candy into a paper sack while he watched.

I handed it to him. He put it on the candy scale.

"You must have quite a sweet tooth," he said. "Cost you a nickel. Or I can put some back."

I was so startled that I just stared at him for a long moment before I held out my dime, warm from my pocket.

"Shall I not put it on Osh's account, as usual?" he said.

I shook my head. "I want to pay for it myself," I said.

So Mr. Higgins handed me the candy, took the dime, and

gave me my change. Then he ran his hand over his face. "Awful hot it's getting to be," he said.

"It is," I said, nodding. Said good-bye. Left the grocery. And headed back toward the bass stands, eating the jelly beans as I went, so lost in thought that I almost tripped over Mouse, who lay sunning herself on the path.

"Mouse," she said, which I took to mean *What's the matter?*

"I don't know," I said.

I thought back to how people always stepped aside when I passed them on a path or the boardwalk. And how I sometimes stepped aside for them instead.

I thought about how people seemed always to keep their distance. And how I always made sure to keep mine.

The schoolmaster, Mr. Henderson, had sanitized the door latch I'd touched. And Mr. Johnson, the postmaster, had wanted to sanitize my letter before he handled it. Two people slow to change. But the others?

"I suppose I ought to think about them one by one," I said to Mouse. But she was too busy chasing a fly to answer.

"What's the matter?" Osh asked me when I crossed to the island and he saw the look in my eyes.

"I think I've been wrong about some things," I said slowly.

He was getting the skiff ready to pull lobster traps. "Like what?"

"Like people," I said.

He huffed. "Easiest mistake in the world," he said. "Go get the basket."

There was a bit of chop offshore, plenty of wind, and it was difficult to navigate our way from buoy to buoy. A struggle to hang on to them while Osh pulled the lobster pots. The skiff wanted to break free, the buoy ropes were slick with weed, and my knees and ribs were sore after just two pots.

"Couldn't we have waited for a calmer day?" I groused as we sailed to the next pot in the string.

Osh shook his head. "Don't like to leave the lobsters in those traps any longer than I have to," he said.

Which made no sense to me. "You think they'd rather be up here, on someone's dinner plate?"

Osh sailed alongside the next buoy. "They're going to end up in a kettle, sooner or later," he said. "Or bait for a striper. No point in spending too long in a trap beforehand."

I snagged the buoy and tied up the skiff as he put it into irons, the sail luffing as it relaxed, some spray coming over the bow.

If I'd been out of sorts before this, I was worse now. "I never looked at it like that," I said. "Makes me feel mean."

Osh laughed a little as he hauled the trap up and into the boat. On a day as windy as this, I kept a post at the buoy rope, making sure it held fast, while Osh emptied the pot. "Not mean," he said as he added another lobster to the basket and replaced the lid. "Just human."

My climb to watch for the *Shearwater* that evening was a relief. I found it hard to be bad tempered on the top of a hill with ocean all around, the western sky like a painting still wet, the wind soft and warm.

Looking for the schooner had become one of my best habits, since it took me up closer to the sky and reminded me that one of my finest days—when I would meet my brother for the first time—was still ahead.

Had I turned to go home just an instant sooner or had I been facing east instead of west, I would have climbed down that hill full of peace and comfort.

Instead, with my last look out toward Penikese, I saw a sail.

A small one.

A skiff, probably.

Leaving Penikese Harbor.

I wondered who it was.

No one from the Elizabeths bothered with treasure hunting anymore. But the skiff was headed for Cuttyhunk as darkness came quickly on. In fact, it seemed to be making straight for me, and I felt my skin tighten.

I watched until it was too dark to see the boat any longer. And then I went home, thoughtful but not yet scared.

Fear came later that night.

Chapter 33

We were sleeping when Mr. Kendall found us. That man who'd left Mr. Sloan to die a slow death for no reason at all.

Had it been a cold, windy night, our windows shut, we might not have heard him.

Had he been more clever, anchoring his skiff in the water, we might not have heard him.

Had we been in a noisy city, we might not have heard him.

Had it been a cold, windy night, had he been clever, had we been in a city, I might have woken to find him leaning over my bed, more terrible in moonlight than ever before.

But it was a warm, still night, and he was a clumsy lout, and we were on an island so small and familiar that we knew he was there as soon as he beached his skiff.

Mouse knew first.

She sat up suddenly, her eyes wide and gleaming in the moonlight flooding the house.

I sat up, too, and turned my head, listening.

From his bed, Osh whispered my name.

"I know," I whispered back. *"I heard it, too."*

Next, the blunt jangle of a sail settling down.

Osh slid out of bed and along the wall to the window facing the beach.

"It's him," he whispered. *"Kendall."*

We had no attic, no basement to hide in, and but one door.

"Osh," I whispered, pointing at my window, which led out the back of the house.

He crossed quickly and opened the old screen as quietly as he could, put Mouse out first, then handed me through, and followed quickly.

Just before he closed the screen again, I grabbed the cinnamon box from the windowsill and pushed it into the sand.

"Hide," I whispered to Mouse, and she slipped away and disappeared into the darkness as if she were made of it.

And then Osh and I crept through the grasses and into the sea, and I clung to him and he to me as the current carried us along the Cuttyhunk shore until we finally broke free of it and struck out toward land, dragging ourselves, gasping, onto the rocks.

"Are you all right?" Osh asked.

I told him I was, my voice shaking. "Are you?" I asked him.

"Come on," he said, pulling me to my feet. "We have to get to Miss Maggie's. Someone told him where to find us."

"Not her," I said. "She wouldn't."

"No, but maybe they told him where to find her, too."

And we stumbled together up the bluff and across the moor toward Miss Maggie, who woke at our pounding and came to the door, wild eyed, and took us straight in.

After we locked the door and told her what had happened, Miss Maggie made a pot of hot tea while I put on some of her shearing trousers and a shirt she wore for gardening, all the cuffs turned back twice.

Osh had to wrap himself in a summer blanket while his clothes dried.

"You'll stay here until morning," she said, "and then we'll call over to Falmouth and tell the police that Mr. Kendall has turned up again."

"For all the good that will do," Osh said. "He'll be long gone by then, empty-handed. Maybe convinced once and for all that he won't find any treasure here."

I thought about the coffee tin. The keepsakes inside it. What they would mean to Mr. Kendall if he found them: the exact opposite of what they meant to me.

I imagined him finding that tin, prying it open, spilling its treasure onto our table and figuring all that it would buy him. The thought made my heart twist. So did the suspicion that he would not be satisfied with such a small amount of treasure. That he would know there was much more, hidden somewhere else. What if he came back for it?

"I kept some on the island," I said in a small voice.

"Some what?" Osh said.

"Some of the treasure. In that old tin you use for seeds. Just a few pieces, before we hid the rest."

"But why?" he asked. "And why didn't you tell me?"

I could hear it in his voice. He was hurt. Sad. And I couldn't have that.

"I wasn't trying to hide it from you, Osh. I promise I wasn't." I looked him straight in the eye so he'd have no doubt about it. "I was going to tell you. I just . . . wanted some of it close by, and you wanted it off the island, and, Osh, I just wanted to make sure I had a keepsake. Something she touched."

"Like the ring you already had? That wasn't enough?"

"No," I said. "It wasn't. If I lost it? If someone stole it? There'd be nothing else."

He shook his head. "You're wrong," he said.

And I knew I was. And I knew I wasn't.

"Even so," I said in a voice that made me cry when I heard it—though I almost never cried, and never before for such a reason—and Osh scooped me up and held my face against his neck until I settled down and sat back, drying my eyes with my hands.

"And there," Miss Maggie said. "Another good reason to call the police first thing. If he's stolen what you set aside for yourself, Crow, he'll need to answer for it."

But Osh shook his head. "We won't tell them a thing about that," he said. "They'll catch him soon enough, or he'll finally run."

"Oh, for Pete's sake," she said. "You can't mean that. He's a criminal. You have to tell them."

But Osh would not be swayed. "How do we accuse him of taking something that's not rightly ours?" he said. "We won't get it back. And they'll look hard at us, Maggie. You know they will. And maybe punish us for taking what wasn't ours to take."

"But it was *hers*," I said. "My mother's. And she left it for me to find."

Osh sighed. "I know that. But I also know how things work."

Miss Maggie looked sad but she did not argue with Osh about that. "He's right, Crow. They won't see it the way you do," she said. "Penikese is state land."

"But that's not fair," I said, sounding younger than I felt.

"Come on, now," Miss Maggie said. "None of us are going to sleep another wink tonight, but we ought to try. It'll be morning soon, and you'll be no good for anything if you don't get some rest now."

She was right. I didn't sleep at all. But I did rest, tucked into her trundle bed, and thought about lots of things as night slipped toward morning. The treasure still hidden, some of it not far from where I lay. My brother, out there somewhere. My parents in their graves on that sad little island. And Osh, lying on the rug in front of Miss Maggie's door, keeping watch even as he slept.

I was so afraid of losing what I had, not sure what I could

both cling to and still reach for. Not sure what I could reach for without losing my hold.

I tried to understand what was really mine to keep or give. Or lose. Or trade away. Or leave behind.

Not so very long ago, I had wanted nothing more than what I already had and, beyond that, only to know where I had come from.

Now, I had much more than before, but I felt most keenly the things I didn't have, especially the parents I'd never known and the brother I did not yet know.

I was stricken, too, by the thought that Mr. Kendall might have found the bit of treasure I'd kept back for myself.

But it wasn't until morning, when we returned to our island, that I understood what he'd taken.

Miss Maggie wouldn't let us leave until she'd fed us a breakfast of dried apples and flapjacks topped with a little honey and cane sugar, and coffee for both of us, which sharpened up our dull edges.

"Our clothes?" Osh asked when we'd eaten all we could.

"On the line," she said, "and still wet."

"Go fetch them," he said to me.

"Stubborn man," she muttered.

"The pot calling the kettle black," he said.

I remember smiling as I went out to the line to fetch our

clothes. I remember forgetting, for that moment, why we had come to Miss Maggie's in the first place.

Dressed again in our soggy things, we walked bowlegged down to the bass stands and across toward our cottage.

From the beach, it looked much as it always had.

I suddenly realized that he could have burned it to the ground, and I felt sick. But I was grateful for the thought, since it reminded me that things could have been far worse than they were.

But they were bad enough.

The door was open, and for a moment I wondered if a huge, angry wind had come through while we were gone.

Nearly everything in our house had been smashed or tumbled. Tables and chairs lay helter-skelter, our dishes broken to bits, everything we owned scrambled and strewn across the floor.

I didn't care a lick about any of that.

That, we could clean up or replace or mend.

But the coffee tin was not on the shelf where I'd left it.

Even worse, even more like a hand on my throat, was how Mr. Kendall had slashed the paintings I'd loved too much for Osh to sell. As if a clawed creature had been here, raging.

And the paints that Osh had so carefully brewed were now splashed across the house in mad streaks, his beautiful clean paper in shreds, the legs of his easel broken.

Osh turned and left the house without a word, but I stayed and stared and felt something begin in my chest.

I'd never hated anyone before.

And I'd never felt so small.

I found Osh sitting in the sand, staring at the ocean, Mouse in his lap.

I sat next to him and waited quietly.

He was still for a long time, not moving except to run his hand down Mouse's back again and again.

Then he said, "None of this is your fault, Crow. But it has to stop."

"I know," I said. "And I'm sorry. I never imagined—"

"Don't," he said. "Not a word. You haven't done anything wrong. But we have to make sure he never comes here again. Ever. Do you understand?"

I nodded. "How do we do that?"

Osh shrugged. "I don't know."

Mouse turned suddenly, staring toward Cuttyhunk, and there came Mr. Johnson, the postmaster, hurrying down the path to the bass stands and waving at us from across the shallow divide. The tide was nearly out, the channel little more than a stream, but he waited on the far side, gesturing for me to come across.

"I have a message!" he called.

We had known from the start that Mr. Kendall was as dumb as he was mean. But we didn't know how dumb until Mr. Johnson delivered the message he had just received on his telegraph machine.

When I crossed over to meet him, he hesitated for a moment and then handed me the slip of paper, curiosity and excitement plain on his face. "Is this about the man from Penikese, who pretended to be the bird keeper?"

I read it, smiling. "Yes," I said.

He nodded thoughtfully. "He was here, wasn't he?"

I looked up at him, startled. "How did you know?"

"Someone was at the inn last night, late, banging on their door, wanting to know where you lived. And they told him. Scared not to. And then they woke me to send a message to the police. Which I did. But then I got to worrying they wouldn't come, or at least not fast enough, so I ran down here and looked across last night, but nothing seemed amiss."

It was a lot to take in, but one thing was clear. Mr. Johnson. His face in the sunlight. The worry in his eyes.

"He'd come and gone by then," I said. "And I'm glad you didn't find him still here. He was very angry."

"But you're all right? And Osh?"

"Yes," I replied. "And Mouse, too."

He waited, hopeful, and I realized that he had questions he was trying hard not to ask.

"We ruined all his plans," I said. "We went to Penikese and ruined all his plans. And set the police on him."

"And made him mad," Mr. Johnson said.

"Very mad," I replied.

He nodded, once, and said, "But all's well now and off I'll go."

As he turned to be on his way, I said, "Will you tell people about the telegram please?" And he said he would, as soon as possible. "Otherwise I might burst."

"Better that people know about him," I said. "In case he ever comes back."

"Not likely now," he said as he headed back up the path and disappeared over the rise.

Chapter 34

I crossed back over to Osh with a glad heart. Mr. Johnson had spoken to me as he would have to anyone. And he had come closer than he ever had.

My head wondered why I cared what he thought or said or did.

But I liked the idea of forgiveness and, by the time I reached our island, dripping with my cold Atlantic wash, I felt lighter than I had in a long time.

"What did he want?" Osh asked.

I read the telegram to him: KENDALL ARRESTED PAWNING JEWELRY. COME TO ASH STREET JAIL, NB, SOONEST. KELLY. STOP.

"Well, that's something," Osh said. "The man's a fool. Pawning those things right off like that. With the police looking for him."

"It's good he's not too smart," I said. "Now we can stop worrying about him."

But Osh didn't seem convinced. "They'll need us, and the real bird keeper, to say it was him we saw on Penikese."

"And here, too," I said.

"No, not here." Osh stood up, brushing the sand from his damp clothes. "They can't know he got that jewelry from us."

"But he would have hurt us!" I cried. "And he ruined your paintings. He should be punished for that."

"I'll paint new ones," Osh said. "They'll put him in jail for hurting Mr. Sloan. No need to tell them about the treasure."

I could see the wisdom in that, but I expected Mr. Kendall would do the telling. "What will we do if he says he got those things from us?"

Osh led the way slowly toward the house. "Let him," he said. "He can't say a word without admitting that he stole them, on top of everything else."

"But if he does tell them, won't they want to know where *we* got the jewelry?"

"Then we tell them the truth," Osh said. "Your mother left it to you when she died."

"Except when they find out that my mother is buried on Penikese, they'll know. They'll say she found the treasure on state land. And then they'll take it away, just like he did."

"Maybe." Osh paused in the doorway. "And then they'll go away, too, and leave us alone."

"But that's wrong, Osh."

He looked at me curiously. "Most of the treasure is still yours," he said. "Worth more than any person could ever need. Why are you so concerned with those few small pieces?"

"Because some rich woman will end up with them and she'll feel like a queen, even though they came from Penikese where she never would have stepped foot. Or sent peaches in the summer. Or figs in the winter. Or soft blankets. Or anything."

Osh sighed. "Time to let that go now," he said.

"I can't," I said. "It's not right."

Osh turned to go into the house. "Maybe not," he said. "But I've said all I've got to say about it." He paused. "Except this: Those lepers were out there for years while we were right here, just across the water. But we never sent peaches or figs or blankets. We never stepped foot out there, either."

I felt like I couldn't breathe. Like my heart had a nail in it. "I know that, Osh," I said, my throat aching.

And then I cried for a long time. And dried my eyes and breathed again and let some of that go.

We stayed in the mess and misery of the house only as long as we had to, trading our wet clothes for dry, finding our shoes, trying not to look at anything else.

I retrieved the cinnamon box from the sand outside my window—achingly grateful that I had that, still—and tucked it in the bottom of our driftwood bin for the time being, though I could not imagine that Mr. Kendall would ever come back.

Then we went to fetch Miss Maggie, who was a witness, too, and waited while she put Cinders and Clover out to graze and got herself ready for the trip.

"This is all very hard to believe," she muttered as we hurried down the path toward the fish pier. "One day, I'm tending sheep. The next, I'm mixed up with a madman."

At the gangway, Miss Maggie bought our tickets. "You can pay me back in lobsters," she said, though Osh always sent some up to her regardless.

We were all three jittery and grim, just hours past a terrible night; but the day was fair, we were together, and Mr. Kendall was caught and jailed where he couldn't hurt us.

Perhaps, as well, I would learn something about the *Shearwater* and whether she had come back to New Bedford or when she might return.

"I wish you could have seen Jason when I did," I said as we stood at the rail and watched the mainland grow and grow. "He saw me just when I saw him. And he looked so much like me, it was amazing."

"You were happy about that, weren't you?" Osh said.

"What, that he looked like me?"

He nodded. The sun behind him made it difficult to see his face.

"Yes, I was happy about that. Why shouldn't I be?"

"Oh, you should, I suppose," he said, though he sounded doubtful. "But that's just one thing: how he looked. Not enough to prove that he's your brother."

I realized what he was saying. "You don't think he is, do you?"

He shrugged. "Maybe he is."

I turned to Miss Maggie.

"I suppose he could be," she said.

But I didn't mind how unsure they seemed.

If it turned out that they were right, I would keep looking. I would find my brother, wherever he was. Mrs. Pelham would help with that.

In the meantime, I would think of that sailor the way I had since I first saw him. As Jason. As my brother. And hope that it was so.

Otherwise, I'd spent far too much time atop the Cuttyhunk drumlins looking for the wrong ship.

We asked a dockhand where the jail was, and he told us straight up Union. So straight up Union we went, block after block, watching for something that looked like a jail. We passed the turn for the hospital, and I was tempted to go back in search of Mrs. Pelham, who knew and loved Jason the way I meant to do. But we had different business that day, and it took us to a big brick building I recognized, immediately, as a jail.

It felt like one, even before we went inside. Strong. Stern. As serious as any building I'd ever seen.

The officer at the desk took us to a windowless room where we waited for a long time, far too hot, and I, for one, began to feel like a prisoner myself. Osh fell asleep, his chin on his chest, and Miss Maggie watched him while I tried not to be afraid of what would come next.

"You got here so quickly," Officer Kelly said when he joined us.

Osh opened his eyes.

"You wrote 'Soonest,'" Miss Maggie said. "This is soonest."

"Well, I'm sorry you had to wait. We were rounding up men who look like Mr. Kendall. It wasn't easy."

"What for?" I imagined a room full of big, ugly, angry men.

"The show-up," he said. "You'll look at a number of men and pick out the one you saw on Penikese."

Osh stood up, Miss Maggie with him, and I said, "Will he have to see us?"

"Ah." Officer Kelly smiled. "Every witness would like to be anonymous. But he already knows you saw him. He's already said some things about you, young lady. And you," he said, tipping his head at Osh and Miss Maggie. "But he won't be able to hurt you. I promise."

"Where's Mr. Sloan?" I asked. "Why can't he do this part?"

"In Maine," he said. "Back home, after what happened to him on Penikese. He'll be along soon enough. His word alone won't be as strong, though, as his and yours both."

Before he took us for the show-up, Officer Kelly stopped in the doorway and said, "You were in the Penikese graveyard last time we saw you."

Miss Maggie nodded. "Tending the graves."

"So you said, but I've been curious about that ever since. Why would you tend those graves?"

"Because they needed tending," she said. "Why else?"

"But why those graves? Why sail all the way to Penikese to tend the graves of people you never knew?"

"My parents are buried there," I said before Miss Maggie could say another word. I would not lie about this.

Officer Kelly almost smiled. "I wondered," he said. "We went back again, Officer Reardon and I. Making sure Kendall wasn't hiding out there. And we found one of the graves all dug up, and a little trunk lying open and empty. We figured he had been there, all right, still looking for the treasure. And had found it. We just can't understand why he had so little loot with him when the trunk was big enough to hold much more."

We said nothing. Osh kept his eyes on the floor.

"Of course, he denies having anything besides what he took to the pawnshop. He claims the jewelry belonged to his grandmother. 'Nothing wrong with pawning what's mine,' he said. But we have our doubts." He looked at each of us in turn. "You wouldn't know anything about all that, would you?"

"Why would anyone dig up a grave?" I said. "Especially where lepers are buried?"

"That's exactly what we asked him," Officer Kelly said. "But he wouldn't say."

They could have showed us a thousand big, flat-faced men, and we would have known Mr. Kendall in a trice.

It was how he looked, yes, but it was also how he looked at us. As if his eyes alone could do us harm.

And they did.

I felt them on me and shivered. This was not a reasonable man. This was not someone who could be made to see sense.

When we all three pointed at him and said "five" for the number pinned to his chest, he lunged at us, screaming, "You'll be sorry!" And it took three officers to hold him back.

"Where's the rest of it?" he screamed as they took him away in handcuffs. "It's mine, and I'll have it! I'll have what's mine!"

Osh stepped in front of Miss Maggie and me. "Come on," he said. "Let's go."

He shepherded us into the corridor and away to where we could no longer hear Mr. Kendall screaming.

We'd already given our statement, back on the island. We'd done what we'd come to do.

So we signed some papers, Osh with an X, and said our good-byes.

"I hope we never see you again," Osh said to Officer Kelly, who unexpectedly smiled. "I hear that a lot," he said. "And I hope so, too. Though you'll have to come to court eventually, to say under oath what you know."

We were mostly quiet on the walk back to the waterfront, the jail and Mr. Kendall behind us, receding.

We considered stopping for a sandwich or a visit to one of

the things the islands lacked: a museum, a theater, a library that held ten thousand books. But all we really wanted was to be on the Elizabeths again, even if that meant facing the wreck of our home.

When we reached the waterfront, I saw the old dockmaster coming along toward us, the smoke from his pipe trailing behind him like a dirty veil, and I hurried ahead to meet him.

"Excuse me, but can you tell me if the *Shearwater* is in port?" I asked.

He squinted at me, his long beard quivering as he slowed to a stop, huffing like a steam engine.

"That I can," he said. "And the answer is no, she's not. Nor has been for weeks, stuck in dry dock in Portland after a run-in with a shoal. But home soon, I expect." He craned his neck to look back down the dock and then again along the waterfront. "One of her cabin boys was here just a few days ago, come back on another ship, but he wouldn't have more to tell you than I have."

So. Not here but home soon. And through the Graveyard she'd come. And I'd be watching.

"Come along, Crow," Miss Maggie said, nodding to the dockmaster as we continued on toward the ferry that was tied up and napping, waiting to be let off her leash again.

And I believe we were all three content as we boarded for the return trip, our duty done, not knowing what was to come next.

Chapter 35

"Storm," Osh said, nearly to himself, as the ferry pulled up to the Cuttyhunk fish pier.

He was looking out across the southern sky as if at a lion creeping closer; but I saw nothing except blue, a few mare's tails on the horizon, though the wind had picked up during the crossing, and the flag on the ferry snapped and strained on its halyard.

"When?" I asked.

He closed his eyes. "Tomorrow," he said. "Maybe late tonight, but by tomorrow for sure."

I took Osh at his word and hoped that the *Shearwater* was not on its way home now after waiting so long to be fit for the sea again.

"Then you'll help me round up the sheep, Crow, will you?" Miss Maggie said, not really asking, sure that I would go with her to bring the sheep into the barn.

"First the sheep, and then the lobsters," Osh said, "and off the water before the wind gets any worse. There's just time for both."

I remembered what he said about not leaving the lobsters in their traps longer than we had to. "Okay," I said. "I hope this won't be a nor'easter."

I rather liked the storms that came rumbling up the coast, but the biggest of the nor'easters were frightening, and we always spent them with Miss Maggie, hunkered down.

"The word from New York is to expect big wind and surf late tonight," Mr. Johnson said when we stopped in at the post office so Miss Maggie could collect her mail. "Lots of rain if it keeps the track it's on. Less if it heads out to sea. But wind either way."

As we walked down the lane toward Miss Maggie's, Osh looked again at the southern skies, his hair blowing away from his face, and said, "The lobsters may have to stay where they are for a bit. Though the storm may take them for a ride."

Sometimes, after a big storm, we sailed out to find that our pots had dragged a good distance. Other times, the buoys broke away altogether, leaving us to dive for the pots on the ocean floor. Or the traps, buoys and all, washed ashore in a broken tangle. But there was nothing we could do about it, short of hauling them all up and in, which we were not about to do.

"If we can't get them today, we'll go out as soon as the storm's past," Osh said.

"Will you come help us bring in the sheep, too, then?" Miss Maggie asked him.

"I don't think they'll come to harm if you leave them out," he said, "but I'll help bring them in if that's what you want."

"My sheep would do the same for you," she said.

And we three spent the rest of the afternoon rounding up the flock from across the moors, Miss Maggie on Clover, until we had herded them all into their pen where they could take shelter in the barn when the time came.

By then we were dirty and sweaty and worn out from the long, strange day.

Osh and I waited at the table under the hornbeam tree in Miss Maggie's yard while she fetched some cold chicken and a pitcher of cucumber water from the icebox, a pan of cornbread, some white cheese.

We sat and ate together as the wind rose and the clouds came up from the south until the sky and sea were both gray and the hornbeam tree began to sway in earnest, the young crows that had nested there long flown by now.

"No lobstering, then," Osh said. "But it's time we went home." He looked at Miss Maggie. "You haven't seen what he did to the house."

"Let me help you set it right," she said.

But he shook his head no. "Bad enough we two have to see it," he said. "You'll just get in a lather."

"I won't!" she said.

But then I saw Mr. Johnson, running down the lane toward

the bass stands, and I yelled out to him, waving, which brought him up short and then back around toward us, calling, "He got away! He got away!" as he ran.

Which made me feel like I was the one who'd been running.

"He got away?" Miss Maggie said. "How could he get away?"

"That man Kendall," Mr. Johnson said as he pulled up and stopped, panting. "He got away." He held out a telegram. "Choked a guard almost to death and escaped."

I read it myself. "The police are worried he might come back here."

"Here?" Miss Maggie snorted. "He'd have to be a lot more than stupid to do that."

"He'd have to be crazy," Osh said.

"More than crazy," she said, "with the police after him and a storm coming on."

"But we've thought that before," Osh said. "And we were wrong before."

"I'm off to tell the others to lock up tonight," Mr. Johnson said, and off he went.

"We'll stay here," Osh said. "Just in case."

"You'll do no such thing," Miss Maggie said. "I'll lock myself in and be just fine. You need to go take care of your poor house. But you come right back here if the storm starts to get too bad."

"We will," Osh said. "If it does. But if you hear anyone knocking, don't open the door until you're sure who it is."

She said she would, and we helped her clean up and put away anything in the yard that might be swept away in the storm.

Then we went on our way, glad to find the tide low enough to cross easily and enough light left in the day to set the house to rights, the broken bits swept into a bin, the furniture set back on its legs.

The lanterns hanging from their hooks were unbroken, and I lit them as the day drew down.

"We'll get to the paint tomorrow," Osh said. All around us, the room was splattered and streaked with red, yellow, and blue. If Osh himself had done it, I might have liked the feeling that I was part of a painting. But Mr. Kendall had done it, in anger, and I wanted to scrub it all away.

"I don't mind doing it now," I said, wetting a rag.

"Tomorrow," he said. "We need to get some sleep now, before the storm comes."

After we had tied the skiff high above the wrack line, we took Mouse inside with us and locked the door and all the windows but the one next to Osh's bed.

"I'll know if he tries to come through there," Osh said. "But I don't expect him back here. Certainly not tonight. And not in this weather."

I lay in my bed, the wind pouring like a river through the room, and tried to sleep.

I knew it was the wind rattling the door against its lock, and not Mr. Kendall, but it kept me awake nonetheless until the sound of Osh softly snoring soothed me into my own sleep. And

I didn't wake until I heard the lighthouse siren singing in the distance and saw the flash of a rocket shot off from Lookout Station, and knew a ship was going down.

I was out of my bed and running before Osh was properly awake. I heard him call my name as I struggled to unlock the door and then pulled it open, the wind pushing it back against the wall, rocking me where I stood.

"Shipwreck!" I called back to him and ran out into the rain and wind, across the beach and straight into the rising channel, so swift now that I nearly lost myself, but then regained my footing and staggered, waist deep, toward Cuttyhunk.

"Crow!" I heard Osh yell behind me, but I kept on, the wind shoving me off balance, the current tugging at my legs, and my nightshirt heavy with water.

Onto the beach I scrambled, gaining speed as I ran past the bass stands and up the lane.

The higher I climbed, the harder the wind tried to take me, the sharper the rain against my face. And then the lifesavers atop Lookout Hill fired another rocket into the wet sky, and I whirled in its light to see where the ship had foundered.

There, back beyond our island, a ship under full sail had come to grief in the storm.

I knew what happened when a ship wrecked. I'd seen it many times. Snatched from their own beds, the lifesavers had by now scrambled for their boats and launched them into the heavy surf, oars churning against the waves, harder and harder until they reached the men drowning in the storm or clinging to their listing ship, its mast snapped short, its sails in tatters.

And then they'd haul the survivors aboard the surfboats and strike out again for shore, this time to a spot below where I was now, down along where the bass stands marked the end of Cuttyhunk. They would come ashore where we lived, just by our tiny island.

From Lookout Hill behind me, another rocket shot skyward, bleaching the night, and I saw the ship more clearly as the sea began to take it under.

It was too small to be a brig or a bark. Too big for a sloop.

I ran.

I ran half blinded by the rain and wind, my feet aching as they pounded the rocky path, down and down to the shore again and along it to the landing place where the surfboats would come.

Osh was there already, as I'd known he would be, waiting to grab me up and shake me. "Don't do that again!" he yelled against the wind. "Don't go into this kind of sea again ever. Do you understand me?"

"It's a schooner!" I cried, pointing east.

And then Miss Maggie came to join us, her hair wild in the storm, her poncho swinging like a church bell, and other islanders came, too, all of them ready to help with those who were hurt or beyond helping, until there were perhaps twenty of us huddled together in the storm.

Miss Maggie wrapped me up in her arms, her poncho snug around me. "I think it's a schooner," I told her.

She laid her cheek against my forehead and said, "I hope it's not."

And I knew what she meant.

I could swim. Like a seal, I could swim. But most sailors—oddly, stupidly—could not.

And I didn't know if a man knocked overboard, stunned, could hope to survive in a big sea, regardless. But I had seen men rescued from worse storms than this. From waters so cold that ice formed on the blades of the oars as the surfmen raced to save them. From wrecks far out on Sow and Pigs Reef, in currents that crossed and tangled to suck the drowning sailors under and spin the surfboats like tops.

Surely every sailor out there would survive a summer nor'easter. Surely no one would die in a storm like this.

Chapter 36

*O*ut of the darkness, the first of the surfboats came at last, the waves thrusting it toward the shore, and we ran into the water to guide it onto the rocky beach.

We helped the weary surfmen and then their passengers, who crouched wide-eyed and shivering in the cradle of the hull.

Most of them were steady enough on their own, needing just a hand to climb out onto the shore despite the bully-wind and the rocking of the boats.

"What's the name of your ship?" I yelled into the wind.

One of them said, "The *Shearwater*."

And I was horrified that I'd hoped for her to come back through the Graveyard when she might have been safely at sea far from here.

I looked across the waves and took heart as another surfboat came out of the darkness.

When it grounded itself on the shore, Osh helped pull it higher up, and I waited as more survivors stumbled out.

None of them looked like me.

I waited, pacing, rain blind.

And then a third boat came surging out of the darkness and onto the sand.

These last sailors had not fared so well.

As I watched, the surfmen lifted the first of them from the boat—a tourniquet on his thigh, his clothes bloody despite the rain and sea—and carried him to a cart waiting on the lane to the village.

Osh and another surfman lifted a second sailor out of the belly of the boat and laid him on a waiting stretcher.

He didn't move.

I pushed my way closer as Osh took one end of the stretcher, the surfman the other, and they headed toward another waiting cart.

Lying on it, his lips blue, his eyes closed, was the young man I'd seen leaving New Bedford Harbor.

"Is he dead?" I cried, Miss Maggie at my side.

"No, not dead," one of the lifesavers said. "Just out cold. Hit on the head and nearly drowned."

Not dead. Not dead. "We'll take him," I said. "Osh, we'll take him, won't we?"

Osh stopped. We all stood there in the rain, the surfmen panting. "Is this him?" he said.

"Yes," I said.

He looked from me to the sailor to me again.

"We'll take him," Osh said. "Until the storm is over at least, we'll take him."

"He needs a hospital." This from a surfman named Mr. Canning, a sailmaker by trade but a surfman, like all of them, with no name but that when a ship wrecked in these waters.

Miss Maggie said, "He can't go to a hospital until the storm is over and the ferries are running." At the doubt on his face, she said, "I know what to do as well as anyone on the islands." Which was true. She did. "And if he needs more than I can give him, we'll take him to the mainland as soon as we can."

"Let's get him settled then," Mr. Canning said, waving at one of his mates to board again, and we put the stretcher across the benches and dragged the boat into the water and climbed in, too, so they could row us the short stretch home and up onto our beach all strewn with weed and flotsam.

"Gently now," Miss Maggie said, and they carried him across the sand and into the cottage.

"Put him in my bed," I told them.

"Down first," Miss Maggie ordered. "On the floor. Straight and flat as you can."

I lit a lamp and watched as, bit by bit, they carefully worked the stretcher from under him and hauled it outside, water streaming off it, off us, and the wind rearranging things as if ghosts were in the house, too, making mischief.

Mouse paced on the mantel, tail twitching, eyes wide.

Then the surfmen returned to their boat without a word and disappeared into the rain, their work done, the sailors saved.

"Fetch some water and some towels and a clean nightshirt," Miss Maggie said, without taking her eyes off the sailor's face. She probed gently through his hair until she found where he'd been hurt. Her hand came away bloody, despite the drenching sea and rain. "And tear something into strips for bandaging his head."

Osh and I did her bidding, quick as we could, and stood watching as she poured the clean water through his hair, washing away sand and strands of sea lettuce, and sponging the salt off his face, a pool forming around him as if he lay in his own private sea.

Osh knelt and carefully dried the man's face and then gently pressed the water from his hair, the towel coming away red, and then held his head a little off the floor so Miss Maggie could wrap it in strips of cloth that had once been a bedsheet.

To Osh, she said, "Help me get him out of these wet things." And I turned away, shivering, surprised to realize that I was in my nightshirt still, drenched myself, my own hair full of sand and salt.

When they began to pull off his heavy clothes, I went out into the night and let the rain wash me clean, tipping my head back, the wind so strong I could hardly breathe, and said, "Don't let him die."

But the wind answered with its customary howl, which I

could not translate, the rain was busy with its endless plunge, and the clouds were in a hurry to be somewhere else.

"Crow!" Miss Maggie called from the door. "Come in here." She left a blanket by the door and went away.

I pulled my wet nightshirt over my head and tossed it aside, wrapping the blanket around me, before I, too, went in and shut the door.

The sailor was now lying in my bed beneath a soft blanket, his breathing slow and steady.

"Why won't he wake up?" I asked.

"He can't," she said. "He's not ready, after that knock on the head. He needs rest, and plenty of it, if he's to get well."

"If?"

"Don't do that, Crow," she said. "He's a healthy young man, and the surfmen pulled him up out of the sea before it could drown him. And they brought him to shore in record time. And now he has us to look after him." She reached out to push the wet hair off my face. "Let's feel nothing but lucky," she said. "All right?"

Osh handed me a towel and a fresh nightshirt. "I'm going to take Miss Maggie home," he said, locking the window by his bed.

"You're leaving?"

"I need some things from home if I'm to care for him properly," she said.

Osh handed Miss Maggie her poncho and put on his own. "We'll be back soon," he said. "You take my bed, Crow."

"You think I'll sleep after this?" I said.

"Try," he said. "It will be morning before you know it."

I stared at the face of the sailor lying so still in my bed.

"He looks like me, doesn't he?" I said.

They both nodded, Miss Maggie smiling. "He does," she said. "Some."

"A lot," I protested. "Doesn't he, Osh?"

"Some. I haven't seen his eyes yet, but he does look like you."

"Even Mrs. Pelham at the hospital said so," I insisted.

"You'll know soon enough," he said. "One way or the other. But don't decide who he is before he has a chance to tell you that himself. Now lock the door behind us."

"You don't think Kendall is out in this storm, do you?" Miss Maggie said.

"He got away before the storm came. I don't know anything about the man except he's a stupid, crazy, monstrous fool. I don't know what to think."

"You'll be back soon?" I said.

"Soon as we can." But then he took a closer look at my face and said, "Perhaps you should come with us."

"But who will watch him?" I asked, nodding at the sailor in my bed.

"He'll sleep for some time," Osh said. "He won't even know you're here."

"Just the same," I said, and I think we both heard the Osh in my voice.

"Then lock the door and don't open it again for anyone but me," he said, running his hand over my tangled hair before he went to take Miss Maggie home.

After they left, I pulled on a clean nightshirt and spent a few minutes looking at Jason—no, Osh was right—at the *sailor*, the lantern light gilding his face, and then in the mirror and then at him again.

When he woke, he would tell me that I was right. That he was my brother. Maybe before morning. Maybe any moment now.

I badly wanted to see his eyes. To know that they could see me.

But I had waited this long. I could wait some more.

I left the lamp burning in case he woke in the night. And I lay not in Osh's bed but on the floor alongside my own, unhappy that the rain on the roof, rapping its wet fingers on the windowpanes, made it impossible to hear him breathing.

But it made sleep easy, and in no time I drifted away.

I must have been very deeply asleep when a thump at the door woke me, suddenly, and I stumbled to my feet, dizzy and half blind with confusion, and realized that Osh was not in his bed but out in the storm.

It was only as I unlocked the door that I remembered.

And by then it was too late.

Before I could shove the bolt home again, the door slammed against me, knocking me to the floor, and Mr. Kendall barged through, the rain and wind with him, as if he were made of storm.

I scuttled out of reach and then gained my feet and backed away until I felt my bed behind me. The sailor was as I'd left him, completely unaware, and Mouse by his side, her eyes fixed on Mr. Kendall.

The windows were shut and locked. I knew I couldn't escape through one of them as we had before. Nor could I leave the sailor and Mouse behind. My only choice was to face him.

"You're too small to be so much trouble," Mr. Kendall said. He shut the door and locked it again. "And too smart to think I'll leave this time without what's mine."

He wiped his wet face with his hand and shook like a dog, rain and seawater flying off him, his eyes red. "Give it to me now and I'll go away and never come back," he said. "I promise."

He took a step closer and stopped suddenly, his eyes on my bed. "What's this?" he said, reaching for the lamp and holding it high. "Is he dead?"

"No," I said. "Shipwrecked. And hurt."

He returned his attention to me. "Where is it?" he said, coming closer.

"I don't know what you're talking about," I said.

"Where is it?" he said more quietly, which was worse than if he'd screamed.

"I don't know," I said. "I don't have it."

"Yes, you do," he said, another step closer, "and if you think someone will come to save you, you're wrong." He smiled. "They aren't going anywhere until I get what I came for."

They. Osh. Miss Maggie. "What did you do?" I said.

He laughed again. "He lay down like a dog when I had her by the neck."

I pictured Osh, bound and tied. Miss Maggie. As Mr. Sloan had been.

"You're a terrible man," I said. "And I won't give you a thing. Not a thing!"

But then he turned the lantern flame up high.

"If you don't," he said, "everything will burn. Everything. Him included," he said, nodding toward the bed. "And you, too."

I would escape, I thought. I was small and fast and I would find a way out. Mouse, too. But not the sailor.

I waited, watching Mr. Kendall's face, his empty eyes, and knew there was no hope for it.

Nothing mattered now except that flame.

"All right," I said. "Put it down and I'll tell you."

"And send me off on some goose chase?" He turned the flame down. "You'll show me," he said. "And if it's not there, we'll come back here together and finish things." He set the lantern aside. "Show me."

Chapter 37

*B*y now, the rain had begun to thin, but the wind was still a wild thing.

Mr. Kendall dragged me out of the cottage and then, when I pointed toward Cuttyhunk, across the channel, gripping my hair in his fist as I led him away from the shore and up the path.

I thought and I thought and I thought as I led him through the dark wind, trying to find a way to lead him somewhere else and not to Osh and Miss Maggie, not back to them, but I couldn't think of a single thing to do except what I was doing now.

I didn't care one bit about the treasure, not anymore, not who touched it, not who took it, except that I did. I *did*. Because of the fist that held me like *I* was the beast, like *I* was the one who needed a bit in my teeth, this man, this bully who had come out of nowhere to hurt us.

Light was starting to seep through the cloud cover to the east, and he urged me on even while he pulled harder. "If you think you can take me into the village, think again," he said close by my ear.

"No," I said. "I'm not. It's where they are."

The path to Miss Maggie's was like a little stream that we traveled too slowly for him, too quickly for me, the house up ahead dark, no sign of anyone. But I knew they were inside, bound and gagged, hurt maybe, and now I was the one to make haste until we were both almost running.

"There," I said, pointing, and he followed me to the table under the hornbeam tree.

Broken branches lay on the ground like bones.

The tree itself swayed and twisted.

"Where?" he demanded.

I tipped my head farther back and looked high into the tree.

"Up there," I said.

He stepped closer to the trunk, dragging me with him, and peered into the branches.

"I don't see nothin'."

"High up," I said. "In a nest. Tied fast."

"In a crow's nest?" Mr. Kendall laughed out loud. "Smart and clever, too," he said. "Maybe I should take you with me when I leave."

I tried to pull away, but he held me tighter than ever. "Up you go," he said, yanking me toward the tree.

"I can't," I said. "I can't reach high enough unless I stand on that table there."

He glanced at the table, knew he'd need to let me go if he were to drag it closer, picked me up instead and hoisted me into the lowest branches. "Get up there," he growled, and I knew how it felt to be free and trapped at the same time, treed by a bear that would follow if he was hungry enough.

I couldn't do it.

I couldn't climb up and throw him the treasure, leaving him on the ground with Osh and Miss Maggie. Once he had what he had come for, he might decide to leave no one behind to sound the alarm.

I climbed a little higher and then stopped on a branch that reached out to one side, nothing beneath it but open air.

"I'm afraid," I said, clinging to the trunk as it trembled in the wind.

"Go on!" he yelled. "Or I'll give you a better reason to be afraid."

But I stayed where I was, whimpering and cringing, while he paced and growled below me, jumping up to snatch at my ankles, but falling short.

"I can't," I cried. "I can't!"

With a final growl of frustration, he dragged the table close and climbed up into the lowest branches.

I waited as he climbed closer.

And closer.

And I jumped.

I hit the ground and rolled straight onto my feet running, running, across the yard and into the house, slamming the door and shooting the bolt as he lumbered after me, bellowing, and threw himself against the door, pounding on it, raging.

And then, suddenly, nothing.

I ran to a window and looked out to see him charging back to the tree and up onto the table, back into the branches as fast as he could.

I had been pretending in the tree. Shaking and whimpering to bring him up with me. But now I began to tremble with real fear, shaking all over as I went to find Osh and Miss Maggie.

I found them in her bedroom, rolled up tightly in wet bed-sheets, like mummies.

When I pulled their gags, they both shouted questions but I paid no attention, unrolling them from the wet sheets and un-binding their wrists and ankles. He had used picture wire torn from the backs of the paintings Osh had given Miss Maggie, and their wrists were bleeding.

Once I'd set them free, I fell back panting and crying on the floor, both of them holding me and each other, too.

"Where is he?" Osh said.

When I told them what I'd done, Miss Maggie tightened her grip. "That was very foolish," she said. "And very smart."

"I thought he had hurt you," I said, my tears like sea-memories on my cheeks. "I thought he would kill you if I went up the tree and threw down the treasure. And me, too."

Osh said, "You did the right thing," and we ran to the window looking out on the yard and the hornbeam tree.

Morning was nearly upon us, the rain little more than a blowing mist, and at first nothing seemed amiss.

But then, as we watched, the big tree began to shake.

I heard a roar threaded through with scream.

And Mr. Kendall came tumbling out of the tree, a large limb falling with him, hitting the ground first, then the big man himself. I swear I felt the impact, though I'm sure it was just the idea of the fall that shook me.

He lay under the tree, unmoving.

"Stay here," Osh said as he unlocked the door, but Miss Maggie and I followed him out into the yard.

"Run and fetch some rope from the barn," Miss Maggie yelled as she ran.

And off I went as fast as I could.

When I dashed into the barn, the sheep scattered in all directions like corn popping.

"It's just me," I said. "It's just me." But they bleated and wailed as I grabbed a coil of rope and ran for the door and across the windy yard to where Mr. Kendall lay on his belly beneath the hornbeam tree.

He looked as mean as ever.

"He's not dead, is he?" I said.

"No," Miss Maggie said.

Osh took the rope and made a lasso out of it. "Come help me," he said, and Miss Maggie held one side of the loop, Osh the other, so they could more quickly slip it around Mr. Kendall's ankles and pull it tight.

He huffed, but he didn't wake.

Osh pulled the rope taut and wound it next around one wrist and then, fast as he could, the other, cinching the two together, the rope surely burning and pinching as he worked.

And Mr. Kendall opened his eyes.

When he tried to move, he found his legs bent up behind him. When he tried to stretch them out, they yanked on his wrists. He made a terrible sound. Like someone was pulling his teeth out. And we all flinched when he began to bellow, but the rope held firm.

"He's too big for us to pull," Miss Maggie said to me. "We need Clover."

Who was sleeping in his stall, the wind, for him, a lullaby.

When we pulled open the Dutch door, he startled and swung his big head around to find out who was up so early.

But he didn't make any fuss at all when Miss Maggie heaved a saddle onto his back and cinched it tight.

"Good boy," Miss Maggie said again and again as she led him out of the barn and into the wind. "Good, good boy."

And he was a good boy until we came up close to Mr. Kendall, who was still bellowing so loudly that Clover dug in his heels and threw back his head.

"There now, boy," I said, patting his cheek. "There now."

"Can I have your kerchief?" Osh asked Miss Maggie.

She gave it to him, and he gagged Mr. Kendall the way Mr. Kendall had gagged them.

And then we three stood and stared down at our giant catch and at one another. I don't know what I looked like, but the two of them were a mess.

"I'm going back to be with the sailor," I said, handing Clover's reins to Miss Maggie.

"And I'm going to tell Mr. Johnson to send for the police," she said.

At the word *police,* Mr. Kendall thrashed harder and screamed wordlessly into the gag.

"They won't be able to cross for a while. Until then, we'll put him with the sheep," Osh said as he tied the end of the rope around the pommel of Clover's saddle.

But first I waved them a little away and said, "He'll talk about this. He'll tell them about the treasure, won't he?"

"Let him. He's a madman. Treasure in a hornbeam tree? They'll laugh. And if they come looking, they won't find a thing."

He was right. "I'll get it down," I said.

"Oh, be careful, Crow," Miss Maggie said, her eyes full of worry.

"I'll be all right," I said. "The tree won't even feel me."

I climbed onto the table and then up into the lowest branches and then higher, hanging on hard.

The tree still swayed a bit in the last of the big wind, and I felt the fear I'd pretended earlier. But up I went, branch after branch, until I reached the bundle of gold and jewels still tied tightly to the tree trunk, all of it hidden by the crow's nest that had held fledgling birds not so long before.

The knots in the wet and swollen rope were loose, and I figured that Mr. Kendall had already struggled with them while the branch he stood on sagged further and further toward breaking. In no time at all I had worked the knots apart and pulled the bundle free, looping the rope into a handle, but ready, if I needed both hands, to drop the treasure to the ground.

Before I descended, I looked out across the yard and saw Osh helping Clover drag Mr. Kendall through the mud toward the barn where the sheep and the pigs and the cows in their stalls, and the rock doves in the rafters, would keep an eye on him until the police arrived.

Miss Maggie, walking backward, waved at me nervously and then tucked her hands beneath her chin. "Be careful, Crow!" she called.

Then down I went, never moving my feet until I had a branch tightly in my grip, down and down and finally onto the tabletop and then the ground, the bundle heavy, my legs weak, shaking a little, as I wondered what to do with it now.

Chapter 38

*G*etting back home to the sailor was more important than hiding the treasure again, so I said good-bye to Miss Maggie and set off down the path, my wet and dirty nightshirt flapping against my legs, my feet bruised and battered, but my hopes high.

Surely the police would be along soon to take Mr. Kendall away once and for all.

Surely the sailor would be awake before the day was done.

I longed for Mouse in my arms, sleep, Miss Maggie's soup, and an hour with no fear in it as I struggled to drag myself and my cargo across the channel and up the beach to our cottage.

The house waiting on the other side was no longer tumbled and tossed, and I myself felt more solid, too, despite the exhaustion that threatened to put me down as soon as I was inside, the door shut, everything peaceful, finally.

The sailor was as I had left him, neither sleeping nor awake. Just still.

Mouse told me that she wanted to roam, now that the storm had moved off to the north, so I let her out and shut the door again.

And felt immediately alone.

It was odd, and sad, but I felt more alone with that sailor lying there than in all the time I'd been waiting for him.

If only he would open his eyes.

I knew if I sat down I would fall asleep, so I went outside, behind the cottage, and stripped off my nightshirt.

The cistern was overflowing with all the rain we'd had, so I spent two pitchers of it on my salty, sandy, weary body.

The water was cold and clean and wonderful, and I felt much better as I stood in the warm wind and thought about the treasure I'd rescued from the hornbeam tree.

In the end, I decided that the cistern would make a good hiding place, at least for a while. At least until I came up with something better. Or gave it away.

I imagined Nurse Evelyn and Dr. Eastman, opening the heavy package I might send, reading the letter inside.

And Jason at the helm of his own ship, a crow on its pennant.

Or, better yet, both. And more, besides.

Once again, and hopefully for the last time that day, I dried myself off and put on some clean clothes, amazed by the power of such a small accomplishment to restore my good mood.

Then I took the bundle out to the cistern, climbed up the ladder fixed to one side, tipped back the lid, and slipped the treasure into the water. It would be easy to see, resting on the bottom of the tank, but only if someone came looking for it.

The sailor was awake when I went back into the house.

He didn't make a sound, but his eyes were open and on me as I crossed the room. They blinked slowly, twice, and then closed again.

I touched his cheek, but he didn't wake again.

He would, though. I knew he would, properly, and soon.

I imagined the look in his eyes. The sound of his waking voice, perhaps a caw as hoarse as mine had been when I'd washed up on this very shore. The smile when he discovered that I was his sister, and he my brother. How happy he would be to have found me, though I had been the one searching.

Osh came through the door soon after.

I'd never seen him so battered.

"Gone," he said. "This time in handcuffs, leg irons, and a hood."

I let out a long, shaky breath that I hadn't known I'd been holding.

"I'm all wet, Crow," Osh said when I put my arms around him and laid my cheek against his chest.

"I don't care," I said into his shirt.

And I felt him sigh, too, as he wrapped me up in his arms and said, "Let's try not to do any of this again. At least not today."

I stepped back, smiling. "Or tomorrow, either," I said.

The sailor woke again later that day. Perhaps the smell of Miss Maggie's soup restored him to his senses. She had brought fresh bread, too, and a spice cake from the grocery.

"Mr. Higgins delivered it himself when he heard about our night," she said, unpacking things from her basket. "Everyone's happy that Mr. Kendall is gone, hopefully for good. They were quite impressed that you helped catch him, Crow."

Which is when I heard the sailor waking. He tried to sit up.

"Lie still," Miss Maggie scolded, hurrying to the bed and gentling him back against the pillow. She laid her hand on his forehead. "Lie still."

He looked at her, his eyes slowly clearing, and at Osh who stood behind us, and then at me.

"I saw you," he said, his voice weak. "On the ferry, I saw you."

I wanted to tell him everything, all at once, but there was time. "Yes, that was me," I said.

His eyes were just like mine.

"Am I on a boat?" he said, looking around at the collection of wreckage that Osh had turned into our home.

"No," I said. "You're on an island. The little one off Cuttyhunk."

"Penikese?" he said, and my heart bloomed.

"No, not Penikese," I said. "What do you know about Penikese?"

"I know to stay away," he said. And closed his eyes again.

Chapter 39

*H*e wasn't my brother.

    I wanted him to be, but he wasn't.

"Your name isn't Jason?" I said. I sounded like Mouse. Small.

"Quincy," he said, "after where I was born, but call me Quinn. Everyone else does."

But I was not anyone else. I had prayed and hoped and believed—really believed—that I was not just anyone else.

I didn't want to be, but I was.

When the sailor closed his eyes again, I stood up from where I'd been kneeling next to his bed.

And I went slowly out onto the beach.

And I sat in the bow of our landed skiff and watched as plovers and pipers stenciled the sand with their quick feet, in search of bugs and baby crabs. As periwinkles etched the beach with their purple trails, and sea foam blew off the waves and tumbled across the beach as if longing for a dog to come out and play.

Mouse came, instead, but she ignored the sea and its foam. Even the birds with their quick feet. Even the periwinkles. Everything but me.

She climbed into my lap and tucked her sleek head under my chin, against my throat where she could hear my pulse and I could feel the small thunder in her chest.

She understood me exactly, as we sat there.

And so did Osh, who had come out to find me just sitting, my face glazed with tears.

"You must think I'm awfully foolish," I said, though my throat had a hard time managing both breath and talk. "You were right all along. He's not Jason."

"You are the one who was right all along," Osh said. He stood next to the skiff and put his open hand on my head. "Nothing wrong with what you wanted."

Mouse wiped my cheeks with her head and then washed her own face, purring all the while.

I tried to smile at Osh, but I couldn't quite manage that. "You said I should be satisfied with what I already had."

He nodded. "I did. And one of the things you already had was a brother. And you still do."

When the sailor named Quinn woke again, he found me, as before, near his bed, waiting to help him heal.

"Why did you ask me about Penikese?" he said.

"Because I thought that's where you came from," I said, straightening his blanket.

"Penikese?" he frowned. "Nobody's from Penikese."

"I am," I said.

And I was stunned when he drew back a little.

But then he caught himself and looked me up and down, and said, "You don't look sick."

"I'm not," I said.

"But you were born there? To lepers?"

"I was born there," I said. "To lepers."

And over the next two days, while I helped Miss Maggie nurse him back to health, I told Quinn some of my story, and why I'd thought he might be my brother.

I did not tell him about finding the treasure.

That, I would save for Jason, if I ever found him.

On the third day, when I knew him well enough, I showed Quinn the tattered letter that had been tucked inside my swaddling when I arrived in that leaky skiff, and told him more about how I had filled in the gaps, with Nurse Evelyn's help.

He studied the letter and the few legible words that remained.

"Read it again," he said, handing it back to me. He settled against the pillows and closed his eyes. "But all of it this time."

"I did read all of it," I said.

"Not just the words there," he said, nodding at the paper in my hands. "The ones that used to be there, too."

I didn't know how I was supposed to do that, but then I

remembered what Osh had said about knowing things, and I looked at those words and imagined my mother writing them or saying them while Miss Evelyn wrote them down, and I thought about how to revive what might have been there before the sea got to it.

Slowly, pausing often, I read, "I would keep you *if I could,* but I don't have any choice except to let you go and hope that someone good-hearted will find you. This letter is all I can give you *for now.* This and a ring for your finger when you're old enough. I *hope you* will think of me when you wear it. I've named you Morgan for a nurse here, Evelyn Morgan, the kindest woman I've ever known. It means *bright sea,* and that is how I'll think of you when you're gone and I'm here without you. I pray that you'll be *better off* than your brother was in the orphanage where they took him after he was born. If you ever come to Penikese looking for signs of me and your father, I hope you'll find the *lambs,* which we carved for you, and the *little feather,* too, to match the one on your face. I hope they lead you to where *I left something* that won't save me or your father or any of us here. But I pray that one *day it might help* you and your brother, too."

I looked up, expecting Quinn to be puzzled at those last lines about something left behind, but he had fallen asleep as I was telling him that story, which was all right with me.

I folded the letter up again and put it in the cinnamon box and took out the ring my mother had sent with it. It was still too big for my finger, but it would fit soon.

And I decided that this was my birthday, whether the calendar said it was or not.

The next day, Quinn was well enough to get out of bed and walk by himself, strong and straight again, so I took him outside for air and a look around.

The remnants of the *Shearwater* had washed up all along the Cuttyhunk rocks and beaches, and a fair bit on our little island, too, including a belaying pin that Quinn now plucked out of the tangle at the wrack line.

"She was not a bad ship," he said. "Not at all." He handed me the pin. "Here," he said. "This should make a fine peg for a hat or two."

I took the pin and rolled it against my palm.

"I'm sorry that I wasn't that brother of yours," he said. "But my own sister will be glad to see me home."

He wasn't trying to be cruel. And it wasn't cruel, really, this truth. That he was not my brother. That he had a sister who · wasn't me.

In fact, I was glad to know something not everyone did: that there are better bonds than blood.

Before Quinn left, Osh gave him some too-big clothes to tide him over until he got home.

Miss Maggie gave him money for the fare to the north shore. "I'm sure you'd do the same for me," she said.

And I gave him the little spyglass I'd carried with me all the while I'd waited for the *Shearwater* to come back. "It's not such a good one," I said, "but it's the best one I have."

Quinn shook Osh's hand and Miss Maggie's. And then he hugged me to him, stepped back smiling, and across to Cuttyhunk he went, bound for the ferry to the mainland, and away.

Mouse mistook my toe for a mole crab, and I used the excuse to duck away and off down the beach to sit by myself for a while.

Miss Maggie went inside, and I hoped she would clear away any signs of Quinn and his stay.

Osh spent some time in the garden, though it was as tidy as a Quaker quilt, and then came to sit beside me.

I didn't have anything worth saying, so I said nothing at all for quite some time.

Osh was quiet, too, waiting.

Eventually, though, a single question insisted that I ask it.

"How do I find Jason now?"

Osh rubbed a smudge of paint off the back of his hand. He'd made a fresh supply and was painting again, which was the thing that finally convinced me we'd seen the last of Mr. Kendall.

I thought Osh might start talking about wild-goose chases or the perils of the wider world, but he surprised me.

"Don't you understand, Crow?" he said, his voice so sad, so tender, that I couldn't breathe. "You're the one worth finding."

Chapter 40

*I*t took us a while to locate the other bundle of treasure, since the storm had dragged it some distance and torn away the buoy that had marked where we'd left it. But I was an able diver and found it one morning in August when the light was just so, the water calm and clear, the lobster trap we'd stashed it in just deep enough that I thought my eardrums might burst as I laced a rope through its slats and struck out for the surface.

Osh, waiting above in the skiff, grabbed the rope and hauled me aboard where I gasped and kicked like a sea robin on a hook.

"Remember," he said as he tied it fast again. "It's the buoy with the extra-long stem."

We agreed to pull it frequently to check on the treasure and to convince anyone watching that it was a true lobster trap and nothing more.

"We won't leave it here through another big storm, though, will we?" I asked.

Osh shrugged his usual shrug. "I suppose not," he said. "But it's really up to you."

And he meant it. I knew that. And I felt taller at the thought.

"Then maybe I'll see if it's meant to be mine," I said.

"And give it away, like you said before?"

"But without such a lot of fuss and mystery."

Osh nodded. "Like sending a baby to sea in a skiff," he said.

I nodded. "Or coming here under a blue sail."

While the treasure stayed safely under the sea, I stayed with Osh and Miss Maggie on the Elizabeths and learned how the stars changed with the seasons, and how we did, too.

Jason never did come there to find me.

I thought about writing to Mrs. Pelham, to ask if he'd been back to see her. To ask if she'd told him about me.

But I didn't.

I was afraid he might have chosen to let sleeping dogs lie.

But I wasn't a dog, sleeping or otherwise, and I still hoped I'd cross his path someday.

Some of the treasure I kept, in case Jason ever did come to find me. Half of it, at least, was his.

And a little of it I held back for me and Osh and Miss Maggie, for when we might really need it.

Some I sent to Miss Evelyn, for the lepers in Carville, Louisiana, along with a necklace just for her. I asked her not to tell anyone where it had come from. To spend the treasure quietly, bit by bit.

With Miss Maggie's help, I wrapped pieces of it in newsprint, tucked them into plain little boxes with no return address, and sent them off to orphanages far and wide.

"You aren't worried that whoever opens these will simply keep what's inside?" Miss Maggie asked as we packed up the treasure in small portions and sealed the boxes tight.

I shrugged. "What would you do if you opened one of these and knew how much food it would buy for those babies?"

"Crow!" Miss Maggie said, her eyebrows high. "You have to ask?"

"Of course not," I said. "And I figure anyone taking care of babies in an orphanage is probably a lot like you."

And if they weren't, there wasn't a thing I could do about that.

At some point during those long, golden years, Osh told me that he'd given me another name when I was new to him.

"Besides Crow?" I asked.

He nodded.

"Besides Crow in your other language?" I asked.

He nodded again.

"What was it?"

"What is it, you mean."

I thought back and back. "Was. Is. Will be," I answered. "It doesn't much matter, since I'm here now. And I have a name." I smiled at him.

"You don't want to know what it is?"

I made a face. "Of course I do, Osh."

So he told me.

It was another of his foreign, musical words, and I vowed to learn how to say this one properly.

"What does it mean?" I asked him.

"Whatever you want it to mean," he said. "I told you a long time ago: What you do is who you are."

I thought back over all I'd done since I'd spied that first fire on Penikese and let it touch a wick inside me.

And I decided that I knew what it meant, that name.

When I said "daughter," he smiled and put his open hand on my head.

"Just like Osh," I said, "means father.'"

A NOTE
ABOUT THIS BOOK

Writing is, for me, the finest possible adventure. All I need is a guide and a place to start. The adventure I took in *Beyond the Bright Sea* began with a young islander named Crow. She simply appeared in my imagination one day, and I spent a few weeks watching her and imagining where she had come from and where she might go next. I knew she would make an incredible guide the minute she introduced me to Osh and their home. And that's when I began to write. The rest came as it came.

I had a wonderful time creating Crow's home on a fictional island off Cuttyhunk. It, and the sea itself, made a magical setting and a strong character, too, interacting with Crow and Osh right from the very beginning. I am a sea person, living on Cape Cod, and am in love with the islands off its shores, so I was able to combine things I know very well with other things I learned by reading about island life in the 1920s. The result is a mixture of fact and fiction: a reflection of that place and time, but not an exact replica.

Likewise, Captain Kidd was a real pirate, and there's evidence that he did bury treasure near the Elizabeths and really did fill Mercy Raymond's apron with treasure when she helped him resupply his ship off Block Island, though none has ever turned up on Penikese (as far as I know).

But all of the other characters in the book—and, especially, the story itself—came completely from my imagination. Miss Maggie showed up nearly at the beginning, and I was pleased to meet her. The same is true of Mouse. I love them both very much. And they fit quite naturally into my blend of real and imagined life on Cuttyhunk.

I've been to some of the other Elizabeths—which also include Nonamesset, Uncatena, Weepecket, Gull, Naushon, Pasque, and Nashawena—so I know them firsthand, but I did a lot of research to learn what they were like nearly a century ago.

Some believe that Shakespeare wrote *The Tempest* after reading the journals of Bartholomew Gosnold, who first visited the Elizabeths in 1602, and that the island in the play is actually based on Cuttyhunk, not Bermuda or Roanoke Island.

Cuttyhunk was, and still is, a wild and isolated place whose shores have many times been littered with the cargo of hundreds of ships wrecked in the Graveyard.

But in the early 1900s, Cuttyhunk was also a summer haven for the wealthy. Famous for its bass fishing, Cuttyhunk attracted businessmen who used carrier pigeons to communicate with their city offices. Whoever caught the biggest striped bass each year was called the "High Hook." Most fished from bass stands on the Cuttyhunk rocks, but the best fishing by boat was around Sow and Pigs Reef, better known simply as the Pigs, named because people thought the rocks looked like a mother pig with her babies. The area is no playground, though. The strong winds, rocks, currents, surf, and fog make it the site of hundreds of shipwrecks, which is why it is known as the Graveyard.

But there is no place in the Elizabeths as serious as the island of Penikese. Learning about that place and its people broke my heart and made me ache for Crow as she struggled, through a confusion of fear and hope, to find her roots.

Like the other islands, the Penikese in this book is a mixture of fact and fiction. At various times in its history, the island was a school of natural history and a turkey farm, among other things, before it became a colony to isolate smallpox patients and then to quarantine people with Hansen's disease, then known as leprosy. Nearly all "lepers" in the United States came from other parts of the world, including Japan, China, Cape Verde, Tobago, Turkey, Russia, and other countries, but any of them living in Massachusetts in 1905 were sent to live together on Penikese, in isolation, as far as possible from everyone else. They were even confined to "the other side" of the island where their cottages and the hospital—and the cemetery—faced Buzzards Bay to the west. None of them was allowed on the side of the island closest to Cuttyhunk.

The residents of the other Elizabeths were so afraid of the

Penikese patients that nannies would scare naughty children by threatening that the lepers would escape and "come get them" if they didn't behave. Only one child was ever actually born in the leper colony on Penikese, and he was quickly sent away to the mainland.

Under the care of a very dedicated and kind doctor and his small staff, the patients were able to spend their best days keeping busy with gardening and other simple pleasures, but fourteen of them died and were buried in the island's small cemetery, leaving behind daffodils and irises that still bloom on "the other side" to this day.

In 1921, after sixteen years of operation, the state closed the colony and transferred its thirteen surviving patients to the federal leprosy hospital in Carville, Louisiana.

A few years after that, the island became a bird "sanctuary," though the game birds and rabbits raised there were shipped to other areas for hunting.

In 1926, when the state gave up trying to sell the buildings and other materials left when the leper colony closed, they burned and dynamited all that remained.

Between 1945 and 1973, no one lived on Penikese, but people still traveled there to hunt, fish, and camp. Penikese later became the site of a school for "troubled boys," which closed after thirty-eight years. Today, it is a residential treatment center for young men fighting addiction.

For me, however, Penikese was and always will be where Crow began her life and where so many others ended theirs.

Like the other islands in this book, Penikese was one thing for those who chose to be there, but something very different for those who had no choice.

Writing this book reminded me that happiness is a matter of being where—and who—we want to be.

Osh and Miss Maggie—even Mouse—and especially Crow understand this truth. For them, an island is the best kind of home. Even better because they are together.

ACKNOWLEDGMENTS

I am grateful to many people for their contributions and support as I wrote *Beyond the Bright Sea*. I am especially indebted to my family—my mother, Mimi McConnell; my sons, Ryland and Cameron; my husband, Richard, and the family he brought with him; my sisters, Suzanne and Cally; and Denise and Ashley Wolk—and in particular my father, Ronald Wolk, who put me at the tiller of a Sunfish when I was quite young and pointed me out to sea without any instructions except to "be careful" and never to underestimate the ocean. The Atlantic taught me everything else I needed to know, and I've been in love with it ever since.

Thanks, as well, to the Bass River Revisionists, a group of splendid writers, friends, muses, and critics who always help me see more clearly what my work needs. Among them, Deirdre Callanan, Susan Berlin, Maureen Leveroni, and Julie Lariviere deserve roses for the care and insight with which they read and responded to an early draft. I thank Patty Creighton, too, for her thoughtful reading and for sharing my work with her husband, Jack, a fisherman whose knowledge of the Graveyard and other waters around the Elizabeth Islands helped me know them, too. I count Connie Rudman and Todd Basch as two other fine readers, and I am indebted to young Zoë Reese Gameros, who read a draft—twice—and shared her reaction with me in a most gracious and helpful way.

My colleagues at the Cultural Center of Cape Cod—Bob Nash, Amy Neill, and Meg McNamara—have been very supportive of my other career, even when I've had trouble keeping all the balls in the air, and for that I am in their debt. My other colleagues, at Penguin Young Readers, are a likewise stellar group. Julie Strauss-Gabel is the kind of editor all writers want: smart, strong, and devoted to words and the power they wield. Her team is the best in the business, and I am grateful for all the expert and devoted people in editorial, design, marketing, publicity, and sales who worked tirelessly to bridge the gap between *Beyond the Bright Sea* and its readers. My amazing agent, Jodi Reamer, is a powerhouse whom I am delighted to have in my corner. She and her associates at Writers House are simply a dream team.

Teachers and librarians like Christopher Brown at Philadelphia Free Library and Literacy Specialist Matt Halpern deserve all our thanks for working so hard to celebrate books and to put them in the hands of young readers. Christopher Rose, Vicky Titcomb, "Totsie" McGonagle, Sara Hines, and thousands of other booksellers across the country and the world are heroes, too. They understand that literature and all arts represent the best of our achievements and the greatest hope for a bright future.

Finally, I would like to thank the doctors and other healers who dedicated themselves to the care of patients with Hansen's disease who were sent to live and, in many cases, die on Penikese. I am grateful as well to the many people who preserved the history of the Elizabeth Islands—recording everything from the kinds of flowers that grew there to the wildlife and the shipwrecks and the habits of the island people—especially I. Thomas Buckley for his thorough and careful book *Penikese: Island of Hope*. I loved writing *Beyond the Bright Sea,* and I am thrilled at the idea that so many wonderful people are behind it. Thank you.

DISCUSSION QUESTIONS

1. At the beginning of the novel Crow asks Osh, "Why is my name Crow?" (pg. 4). Do you know the origins of your name? What does your name mean? In what ways is your name part of your identity? If you could name yourself, what name would you choose and why?

2. Crow is both Crow and Morgan. She is the daughter of Susanna and Elvan, as well as Osh. Osh is also Daniel. He is a painter, a father, a fisherman, and a foreigner. How do Crow and Osh harmonize their different identities? In what ways do these roles shape their lives? Do you have more than one role or identity? How do the different parts of you fit together to make up who you are?

3. Why do names have such profound meaning for Osh and Crow? What physical and behavioral characteristics does Crow share with her feathered namesake? If you were named for an animal, which one would it be and why?

4. Crow says on page 7: "When I asked questions about pearls or tides, [Osh] did his best to answer them. But when I looked beyond our life on the islands, he became the moon itself, bent on tugging me back, as if I were made of sea instead of blood." Why is Osh so reluctant to talk to Crow about her past? Do you feel he is right to withhold information from Crow? Explain why or why not.

5. Why do you think Crow needs to know where she came from? Do you think she would have been better off not knowing? Explain why or why not.

6. The island itself could be considered a major character in the story. Describe the "personality" of the island. How does the island interact with the other characters and influence their actions?

7. Crow believes that her parents set her adrift because they perhaps felt as if they had no choice, that ultimately they were doing the best thing for her future. Do you think that we always have a choice in what we do? Why or why not? Are there circumstances that could limit someone's choice in a situation? Give some examples.

8. "What you do is who you are," Osh tells Crow (pg. 75). What do you think he means by this? In what ways can your actions and behavior become part of your character? Is it a good or bad thing, or can it be both?

9. How do the people in the community react toward Crow? How does fear affect their behavior? What is Crow's reaction to the way they treat her? Do you think the reason for their behavior toward Crow is acceptable? Why or why not?

10. Osh says, "I ended up here because my country was not really my country. It was just where I lived. Where some of us were less than others. Where it was sport, to hurt us" (pg. 87). What do you think happened that caused him to leave everything behind? What challenges did he face when starting a new life on a small, isolated island?

11. It is clear that by moving to the island Osh not only left everything he hated behind, but also the things he loved. He had a family in his past before Crow. Do you think you could ever leave behind your family? What circumstances can you think of that would make someone leave their family and friends behind?

12. Both Crow and Jason started off at the same place. In what ways were their lives shaped by where they ended up—Crow with

Osh, and Jason at the orphanage? In what ways were their lives shaped by where they started, on Penikese with the lepers?

13. How has Jason shaped Crow's life although they have never met?

14. Why did Crow want to keep some of the treasure her mother left behind? Why did she hide it from Osh?

15. Osh did not give the police his real name after some of the treasure was stolen from their home, and he also seemed to be wary in their presence. Do you think Osh could be hiding from something or someone from his past? Do you think Osh is capable of doing something bad? Use examples from the text to support your answer.

16. In your opinion, do you think who Osh was in the past matters? Or do you think all that matters is who he is now? Explain why.

17. Osh was worried that the treasure would change Crow. Why was he so worried? In what ways do you think gold or money could change a person? What would you have done with the treasure if you had found it?

18. In the end, Crow was not able to find Jason. Do you think she ever will? Do you think Jason wants to be found, or would he like to leave his past, including Crow, behind him? Explain why you think this.

19. Crow comes to the realization that "there are better bonds than blood" (pg. 278). What do you think she means by this? How did she come to this conclusion? Do you agree with Crow? Why or why not?

Turn the page for a preview
of Lauren Wolk's new novel,
Echo Mountain

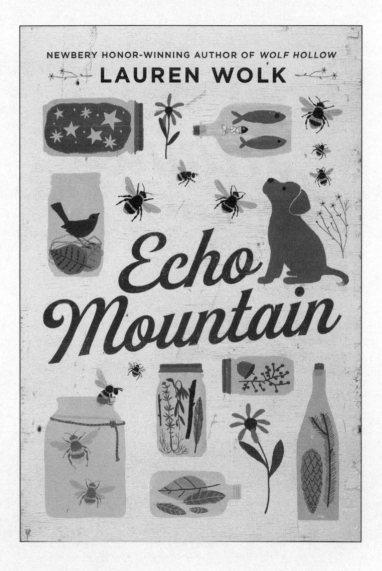

NEWBERY HONOR-WINNING AUTHOR OF *WOLF HOLLOW*

LAUREN WOLK

Echo Mountain

Maine

1934

Chapter One

The first person I saved was a dog.

My mother thought he was dead, but he was too young to die, just born, still wet and glossy, beautiful really, but not breathing.

"Take him away," she said, sliding him into my cupped hands.

Her voice was cold. Perhaps that was why it shook a little.

But I knew her better than that.

Maisie, curved around her three living pups as they poked blindly toward her milk, watched me with aching eyes.

I could feel how much she hurt, too.

"What should I do with him?" I asked.

"Bury him far beyond the well." My mother turned to tidy the bedding straw. It was as red as Christmas. We'd all had a hard night. But it had been hardest for the last of the pups. The one in my hands.

I cradled him close against my chest as if I had two hearts but only one of them beating, then carried him away from the wood-shed, into the pale spill of morning light. Past the cabin, toward the well and a grave waiting beyond it.

But then I stopped.

Looked back.

And there, on the cabin's broad granite step: a wooden pail brimming with cold water, waiting to be useful.

I didn't know what was about to happen, but a little flicker in my chest flamed at the sight of that water full of green and blue from the tree, the sky overhead. Calm. Simple. It spoke to me with a voice louder than my mother's as she stood at the door of the woodshed, bloody straw bundled in her arms, and said, "Go on then, Ellie."

But I didn't go on then.

The flicker, the flame, the voice all tugged me toward the bucket, where I plunged the baby dog deep into the cold, cold water and held him there until I felt him suddenly lurch and struggle.

"Ellie! What are you doing?" my mother said, dropping the straw and rushing toward me.

But she stopped and stared when I lifted the dripping, squirming pup and pulled him back against my chest.

"He's not dead," I said, smiling. "Not dead at all."

Which made my mother smile, too, for just a moment.

"Then he's yours," she said, turning back for the straw. "See that you keep him that way."

I didn't know if she meant that I should keep him alive or keep him mine, but I intended to do both.

I sat on the step and dried the pup on my shirttail, roughing up his slick pelt, which made him breathe harder—which made me breathe harder, too, a series of sighs, as if we'd both been starved for air.

Then I took him back to Maisie, who lifted her head and watched as I wedged him between the other pups and showed him the teat meant for him.

When Maisie laid her head back down again, she sighed, too.

The pups all looked mostly the same. Dark. Perfect. One of them had a white forepaw. Another was bigger than the rest. Another, some color in his coat. And my boy had some brindle, too, and a white tip to his tail, as if it were a brush he'd dipped in paint. So that set him apart.

But I didn't need a marker.

I was sure that I would know him again in an instant. And I was sure that he would know me.

"I'll have to think of a name for you," I told him as he began to gulp down his new life.

And I did just that all through my morning chores.

While I pulled winter grass from the potato patch, I decided against *Shadow* (though he was dark and it suited him).

I thought of *Possum* (because he hadn't really been dead, not really) as I bundled the grass and set it aside for the cows.

I considered *Boy* (which he was) and *Beauty* (which he also was) as I weeded early spinach come up from autumn seed.

I thought about *Tipper* (for that white tip) as I bundled kindling.

And finally—while I stowed the wood in the bin by the big kitchen stove—chose *Quiet.*

My little brother, Samuel, said, "I like that," as we ate a breakfast of dried blueberries, fire-black potatoes, and milk still udder-warm. "It's a heartbeat name."

My mother said, "A what?"

"A heartbeat name. You know: two parts. *Ba-bum. Ba-bum.*"

And *I* liked *that.*

Esther said, "Quiet's a dumb name." But she was my big sister and thought everything I did was dumb. "He'll wander off somewhere and you'll go yelling 'Quiet!' at the top of your lungs." She shook her head. "Dumb."

But I disagreed, though I did think that Quiet was an odd name. Which was all right with me.

I myself was odd in many ways, and I liked other things that were odd. Questions worth answering. Like the ones that would soon lead me to Star Peak, to a boy who could make a knife sing, to a hag named Cate, and the other *else*s I came to know during that strange time. Some of them good. Some of them bad. All of them tied to the flame that burned more brightly than ever on the day when Quiet was born.

Chapter Two

Quiet's grandmother, a sweet dog named Capricorn, had started her life as I had started mine—in a town where my father was a tailor and my mother a music teacher, before the stock market crash that made almost everyone poor and sent us to live on Echo Mountain.

"But who crashed?" I had asked my father when our own lives began to spin toward disaster.

My father told me that too many people had gambled with their money and then panicked when it looked like they might lose it . . . which, in fact, made them lose even more, and made them poor, and us along with them.

"I don't understand." I remember looking up at him, expecting a better explanation than that. "Did we gamble with our money?"

He shook his head.

"Then why did we lose ours, too?"

"Not ours, right off. But people who have no money don't pay a tailor to make their clothes, and they don't buy new clothes when the ones they have will do."

My father was more than a fine tailor. His clothes fit us like second skins. And the vines and flowers he stitched into his hems and cuffs were more than beautiful. They were like signatures. Like signatures on paintings.

"But Mother is a teacher," I said. "Do you mean that people are too poor now for school?"

He shook his head again. "No, I don't mean that. Quite the contrary. More music right now would do everyone a world of good. But I'm afraid music is one of the first things to go when a school is in trouble. And we're not the only ones leaving. Half the town has gone away, moved in with kin, or just . . . moved. To live on the road, in the rough, looking for work. Which means not so many children in the school anymore. And no need for all the teachers they once had."

No need for my mother.

And so we lost his shop first. And then our house. And then the life we'd always known.

Which was when I understood the other name that people used when they talked about the crash. The Depression, they called it. The Great Depression. Which meant something dreadful and dark.

I didn't need my father to tell me that. It was in my mother's face. My sister's face. Somewhere more distant than that, in my father's eyes, but there all the same.

We took Capricorn with us when we left town, though we didn't know how we'd feed ourselves, let alone a dog.

When we arrived at our little portion of mountain, we tied up our new cows, piled our belongings under a canvas to save them from the weather, and lived in a crooked tent while we built our cabin.

Poor Capricorn was baffled by our new life in the woods. She had always been happiest under the kitchen table while we ate or at the foot of a bed or in the garden we'd had before the crash. But we had no kitchen anymore, no kitchen table, no garden to give her comfort, so we took her into the tent each night, where she managed to give *us* some comfort instead.

It was Capricorn who growled warnings in the night when a bear came close, sending my father out with a torch to scare it away.

It was Capricorn who trembled and cried so hard when thunder came that we all felt brave in comparison.

And it was Capricorn who brought me the strangest gift I'd ever received: a tiny lamb, carved out of wood, tied with a bit of twine to her collar.

"What's that?" I said when she came through the trees one morning, already skinny, learning to hunt for the first time in her life, much as my father was. But she had a choice between field mice or bean soup, so hunt she did.

I untied the little lamb and held it up to the light.

"Where did you get this?" I looked her in the eye, but she had nothing to say.

I peered into the trees all around me but saw only my father, cutting popple. Esther, gathering firewood. My mother, lugging a pail of water up from the brook, Samuel clinging to her skirt.

No one else.

We had come to know the other four families that settled nearby. They were all good, solid, hard-boiled Mainers who saved bits of string and sucked the marrow from their soup bones. None of them would have dulled their knives with such whimsy.

But Capricorn would not have let just anyone get close enough to tie something to her collar, so I judged that one of those people must have carved this little gift and sent it home with her. Who else?

Perhaps they had hoped that Samuel would find it.

But I knew he would lose it in the mud.

And it felt like it was meant to be mine.

So I stashed it in the toe of a church shoe I was unlikely ever to wear again. And told no one.

If anyone was going to unravel its mystery, I wanted it to be me.

Chapter Three

We spent our first spring on Echo Mountain damp and dirty and tired, as hungry as the animals that crept from their burrows after months of winter fasting.

Building a cabin was our work, our play, our church and school. The other families helped us with the heaviest parts, just as we helped them, but most of it we did ourselves, and so slowly that at times I thought we would never again have a roof over our heads.

Samuel was too small to help much, except by making us laugh and love him, which was plenty. Sometimes that's all a person needs to do: be who they are.

Esther and my mother worked as hard as they could, their soft town hands ruined, their hair a mess, and they cried at night when we lay down to sleep. They seemed to blame the mountain itself for what people had done.

Every shrieking storm reminded them of the day my mother had lost her job: the last goodbyes to the students she'd come to think of as her own children.

Every coyote that howled us awake reminded them of the day my father had closed his shop, his face like a wet stone, everyone too poor now for his beautiful clothes, for the ivy he embroidered through every hem and cuff.

And every long, gray rain that found its way into our sad tent reminded them of how we had lost our house. Sold nearly everything we owned. Took what little was left. And went looking for a way to survive until the world tipped back to well.

But I didn't blame the mountain. It was, after all, what saved us.

For the first few weeks, we lived on a watery soup of beans and salt.

We ate rabbit when my father could kill one, but he was a slow and clumsy hunter in those early days, and the rabbits of Echo Mountain were fast and clever, so we were far more likely to eat turtle when we could.

But neither my mother nor Esther ever took to possum, which was easy to catch but greasy and gamey and tasted like whatever the possum itself had eaten. A hungry possum will eat almost anything. But a hungry person will, too, so possum we ate when possum we had.

It was hard. All of it. Especially for my mother and my sister, who lived in a brew of fear and exhaustion, lonely for the life they'd left behind.

My first spring on the mountain was a kinder season.

Like my father, I loved the woods. From the start, the two of us were happy with our unmapped life. The constant brightness of the birds. The moon, beautiful in its bruises. The breeze that set the trees shimmering in the sun, fresh and joyful. And the work we did together to build ourselves a home.

For every difficulty, there had been some kind of good work we could do. So we'd done it.

But this bond with my father and the wilderness itself made a rift between me and my mother—and my sister especially—who both seemed to think I had somehow betrayed them by being happy when they were not.

Nothing about life on Echo Mountain was harder for me than that rift: the idea that I should be sorry for being different. And I made up my mind early on that I might miss my mother, miss my sister, and be lonely, but I would not be sorry for what set me apart.

I loved the mountain. And I loved what it kindled in me. And that was that.

But it wasn't easy.

If I needed another reason to love where I was, I got one on a morning in May when the whole world hummed and the air was sweet with the first of the lilac.

I found it in the pocket of my jacket, which I'd hung from a tree branch and forgotten.

My father had made that jacket in his shop before the crash, stitched it with spring flowers, carved the buttons from hardwood, made it with plenty of room for me to grow. And I wore it whenever

I could, through work and weather and mess, while Esther and my mother kept theirs packed in brown paper, safe from harm, and scolded me for every new rip and stain.

When I plucked my jacket from the branch and slipped it back on, I found in the pocket a perfectly carved snowdrop sprouted from a bulb, so fine and delicate that I lifted it to my nose, expecting a whiff of meadow.

This time, I didn't turn to search the woods around me.

This time, I let my eyes look past the carving and into the trees.

And there, just in that thicket there: a face.

Framed by leaves, as if it were part plant itself.

And then gone.

I blinked. Looked harder.

"Hello!" I called, but no one answered.

So I slipped the snowdrop back in my pocket and spent the rest of the day wondering about that face. Those eyes. Watching me.

After that, I looked more closely at the faces of the others on that mountainside, peering at them thoughtfully until more than one said, "Is there something in my teeth?" Or, "My wife has an old pair of glasses that might suit you."

But none of the faces looked like the one I had seen. They were all too old. And none of them had enough . . . loneliness in them. So I went on as before, working hard, learning so much every day that I thought I might pop like corn in a kettle, and watching the woods to see who might be watching me.

When the first room was done, we moved out of the tent and into the cabin.

I remember: It was June and we were no longer cold except at the very darkest part of night.

For me, that was enough.

But my mother and Esther made my father put a bolt on the cabin door, so they could lock us in each night and sleep, finally, in peace. Dry. Safe. A thick wall between them and the wilderness.

By the time our first mountain winter came, we had a snug, safe home with four good rooms—one for us children, one for our parents, one for our kitchen, and one for everything else. A root cellar for what we'd grown the whole summer long. A place where we could start again. The know-how to make our way in this new world. And, for some of us, the blessing of knowing that we were blessed.

But that was before my father's accident changed everything.